Nikos swallowed a laugh.

"A race," he repeated. "Yes. A Grand Prix. You're not a racing fan, huh?"

Olivia shrugged. "No. I'm not much of a sports fan in general. I'll go to a baseball game, but that's more for the vibes."

A look of horrified comprehension washed over her face. "Oh, I see your shirt. I'm so sorry. You live here. I bet you're a big fan. I'm not trying to be rude. I'm sure it's a really cool sport. A great time. No offense."

"None taken." He smiled. "But back to your cookies. I've got a bike. We can get around the barricades."

"A bike, huh?" She tilted her head.

Say yes, say yes, his heart thudded.

Unbidden, he imagined her arms encircling his body...

She blushed as if she could read his thoughts. Or was she having similar thoughts of her own? Either way, she didn't appear to be put off, which was encouraging. But he still wasn't sure she would accept. There was uncertainty, and he wasn't used to uncertainty with women. This was a challenge. He liked challenges.

Dear Reader,

Life has a funny way of coming full circle.

Formula 1 racing snuck up on me. For all the years I've known my husband, he's been a fan. The whiny shriek of high-powered engines frequently permeates my dreams during Sunday race-day naps on the couch. We attended the inaugural Indianapolis Grand Prix in 2000, and I had the thrill of doing a "hot lap" at the Porsche driving school at Road Atlanta. Who knew these experiences would provide the context for my first novel?

When the Billionaires Wanted pitch appeal appeared in my inbox, it was a no-brainer for my Greek billionaire to be an F1 driver. Monte Carlo was the perfect place for a glamorous destination wedding, not to mention an iconic race. Of course, being a lifelong Pittsburgher, I believe no wedding would be complete without a cookie table! This all comes together in the story of Nikos and Olivia.

I'm delighted by the opportunity to write for Harlequin. While I dedicate this book to my grandmother, Meme, who loved a good "beach read," I also appreciate my favorite idea partner and toughest critic, my daughter Steph. Someone needs to keep me in line.

Elle Brown

BRIDESMAID'S FAST-TRACK FLING

ELLE BROWN

ISBN-13: 978-1-335-47073-7

Bridesmaid's Fast-Track Fling

For questions and comments about the quality of this book, please contact us at CustomerService@Harlequin.com.

Harlequin Enterprises ULC
22 Adelaide St. West, 41st Floor
Toronto, Ontario M5H 4E3, Canada
www.Harlequin.com

HarperCollins Publishers
Macken House, 39/40 Mayor Street Uppe
Dublin 1, D01 C9W8, Ireland
www.HarperCollins.com

Printed in U.S.A.

Elle Brown is a creative polyglot. She is a romance writer, painter, digital communicator, web designer, speaker, costume-maker, camp director and pied piper. Regardless of title, the common denominator in every endeavor is that Elle is a storyteller. A Pittsburgh native and Carnegie Mellon graduate, her greatest joy is hosting epic meals in which her husband cooks, she designs fantastical tablescapes and their dog blisses out on leftovers. With all her heart, she believes that everyone deserves a happily-ever-after. Find her at ElleBrownAuthor.com.

Bridesmaid's Fast-Track Fling
is Elle Brown's debut title for Harlequin.

Visit the Author Profile page at Harlequin.com.

For my grandmother, Meme,
who said I would write books. So I did.

SUNDAY MORNING

"GOOD MORNING, FOLKS. This is your captain speaking. As we make our final approach into Nice, we've got some bad news..."

Olivia Keller picked her head up from her travel pillow and frowned.

Just in case they were about to attempt a water landing, she popped the AirPod out of her right ear to hear the rest of the pilot's announcement. She promptly dropped the earbud between the seats, likely never to be seen again. Money lost before she'd even landed.

"...unfortunately, the anticipated French transportation strike began this morning while we were in the air. This may cause a delay in reuniting you with your checked baggage. We apologize for the inconvenience. We'll be on the ground shortly. Welcome to France."

Despite the discouraging news, Olivia eagerly pushed her face against the window. Her first glimpse of the French Riviera was spectacular. She marveled at the gradients of teal-and-turquoise water encircling Côte d'Azur Airport as it came into view.

"Damn."

It wasn't as if she had never traveled or seen the sights. She'd spent a semester abroad and partied her way through some of the most beautiful cities in Europe. But her shenanigan days were done. At twenty-six, she was a professional analyst at an exclusive New York City firm. She was categorically too old and blasé to be awestruck.

That being said, this trip was a fresh start. A big, exciting reset button. She'd recently put an end to a situationship that had dragged on for far too long. It was absolutely the right choice; she wasn't heartbroken over Sebastian. At all. She'd simply decided that, realistically, he wasn't worth it. Like every man she'd ever known—starting with her father—he wasn't worth her time or energy. Certainly not her heart.

But now, looking out the plane's window, seeing the Mediterranean so vivid that it seemed unreal…it stole her breath. Instant magic. It gave her a tingly feeling, like a premonition that something incredible was about to happen. Maybe the protective shell hardened around her heart might have a tiny crack. Maybe she might be open to new and unimagined possibilities unattainable in her daily life in New York. Maybe once she landed…

Or not. If there was anything that could kill a magic buzz, it was navigating a French airport during a transportation strike.

After finally clearing customs, Olivia stood at the unmoving baggage carousel alongside fellow passengers who had been foolish enough to check a bag on the eight-hour flight. She waited. Nothing happened.

This situation required professional intervention. She approached a nearby glass-fronted office.

"Bonjour, Madame." Olivia knew the French valued politeness. "I was on the New York flight… there is no luggage yet at the baggage claim."

The perfectly coiffed woman behind the counter did not look up. She kept typing, her lacquered nails clickety-clacking over her keyboard.

"*Non*. It is not here." The woman shrugged. *"Très désolée. Je ne sais pas."*

She didn't know. Okay. Helpful.

With no clear answer, Olivia gave up on her checked bag and set off through the terminal to determine if the economy bus she'd pre-booked to Monte Carlo was still running. She had a feeling that it wouldn't be.

Her fears were confirmed. Handwritten signs on the bus, tram, and taxi kiosks included three critical French words, written in bold: *Grève des Transports*. Transportation strike.

In her sleep-deprived state, she was definitely not coherent enough to figure out how to get herself from Nice to Monaco. A text popped up before she could devise a plausible solution.

Have you landed?

Her frustration vanished, if only temporarily.

YES!!!!!! I'm HERE!!!! But not sure how to get to Monte Carlo. Everyone on strike

Her phone buzzed.

"Oh my God, what is happening?" Olivia's favorite voice in the world bounced across the airwaves.

She spent the next five minutes explaining her travel woes to Maggie, her best friend since forever and the soon-to-be bride. During their European adventures, Mags had met her now fiancé, who happened to be a Swiss-banking genius. It was their wedding that drew Olivia across the pond to Monaco.

She heard someone murmuring to Maggie in the background.

"What about a helicopter? It's a quick seven-minute flight. Easiest way to get here," Mags suggested. "Stefano's Uncle Klaus and Aunt Kiki might still be at the heliport…you could hitch a ride with them on their helicopter…oh? No?" Maggie resumed a muffled conversation with the unseen third party.

"Klaus and Kiki?!" Olivia couldn't help laughing. "Those can't be real names."

"Those are indeed their real names, but it doesn't matter. Klaus and Kiki have already arrived in Monte Carlo," Maggie said. "I'm here with my wedding coordinator. She'll call the concierge at the Hotel Negresco in Nice and arrange to have someone give you a ride. The car can pick you up at the airport and take the scenic route along the coast. It's amazing. You'll love it."

"Okay," Olivia hated to ask, but… "Mags, any idea how much this will cost me…?"

"Stop," Maggie insisted. "I'll add it to the wedding tab. It's fine."

"You already covered the cost of my room!"

"Because I can't get married without you. Also…" Maggie's voice dropped to a whisper, presumably so the wedding coordinator wouldn't overhear. "… I have a job for you."

Two hours later, a black Mercedes limo rolled Olivia in style to an ornate Belle Époque palace, the iconic Hôtel de Paris Monte-Carlo. She had expected to doze during the ride, but the breathtaking scenery was enough to keep her wide awake, gaping out the window. Mags hadn't lied—the sea vista on one side and medieval French villages on the opposite cliffs were straight out of a fairy tale.

She had imagined strolling the glamorous Casino Square, but that would have to wait. Utter exhaustion washed over her. Climbing the stairs under the imposing alabaster sculpted entrance, she had one goal: hit the bed and get some sleep.

But she hesitated inside the glass-domed lobby. The magnificent space, with its marble floor, golden pillars, and gigantic floral arrangement, was opulent beyond anything she'd ever experienced, even in New York City. She watched four impeccable women walk through the lobby, each carrying a Birkin bag. Apparently, Monaco was one big Hermès meetup.

She'd planned to change out of her travel sweats before leaving the airport. Sweats were obviously too casual—plus her top was stained with a dollop of mustard from the hot dog she had eaten in the cab on the way to the airport. It wasn't her best look.

Unfortunately, her carefully curated outfits were all stashed in the missing suitcase. She had pajamas and a bathing suit in her backpack, but neither seemed a good option for her Monte Carlo debut.

Olivia nonchalantly tugged loose her travel bun to allow her recently highlighted hair to tumble over her shoulders. She hoped it would give her movie-star-sexy tumbled-out-of-bed vibes, although she suspected her look was more like a witch caught in a windstorm. But there was nothing to be done at this point. She just needed to escape the lobby as quickly as possible. She approached the front desk, ready to bluster through.

"Olivia!"

Olivia twirled toward the greeting, delighted that Mags didn't care that Europeans generally didn't shriek indoors unless they were watching soccer. Maggie tackled her in a crushing hug, and Olivia could barely keep upright against the aggressive greeting.

"It is so good to see you! I know we talk constantly, but it's not the same. You're here!" Maggie exclaimed. "You're *here*."

"I'm here," Olivia confirmed. "Just a little worse for the wear. It was a long trip. Long day. I've been up since yesterday morning, five o'clock."

"Your hair looks really good, though."

God, Olivia loved this girl. There was a reason they'd been friends since birth.

"Thanks. And look at you, the blushing bride!" Olivia choked up a little as she spoke.

Then she remembered Maggie's odd, secretive comment on the phone. "So, what's this job you need me to do? Tell me so I can go get some sleep."

As the room key was obtained, Maggie explained. "Céline, the wedding planner who arranged the car to get you here… She's amazing at handling all the wedding details. She's Swiss, so she's totally on top of it. Like clockwork, as they say."

"But?"

Mags sighed deeply. "The cookie table."

"A cookie table? You are going to have a cookie table?!" Olivia questioned, linking her arm through her friend's elbow as they moved through the lobby.

"*Of course* I'm going to have a cookie table."

In Western Pennsylvania, where they had grown up, most weddings included a cookie table during the reception. But Monte Carlo wasn't Pittsburgh.

"So what's the problem?"

Mags shut her eyes and took a deep breath. "The hotel catering—which is fabulous, world class—doesn't really do cookies. They do cakes and pastries—amazing French things that I can't pronounce and taste divine. But that's not what I want. I want homemade cookies like my mom and grandma would have made if they were still with us. I have their recipes. I keep trying to explain to Céline. But she's being weird about it. She doesn't get it."

Her face turned wistful.

"Liv, ever since we were little girls and went to your aunt's wedding…"

"We planned our dresses and our honeymoons. And we planned out every variety of cookies we wanted on our cookie tables," Olivia remembered.

"Exactly!" Mags confirmed. "I still have the list."

"You do recall that we were supposed to have a double wedding…" Olivia teased. "I guess that part of the plan fell through. You didn't bother to wait for me."

"If I waited for you, I'd likely be waiting forever." Maggie raised an eyebrow. "Last I checked, you'd sworn off any possibility of happily-ever-after."

"Love 'em and leave 'em. And definitely don't trust 'em. Still true," Olivia confirmed.

As a friend, Maggie had helped Olivia survive every lie, betrayal, and rejection her father had dished out over the years. Through cycles of disappointing boyfriends and dead-end relationships, Maggie understood why Olivia had never been willing to fully open her heart, why she'd never let any guy get close enough to do any real damage. Olivia didn't need to reiterate why the likelihood of her traipsing down the aisle was slim.

Maggie shrugged. "Someday you might sing a different tune. For your sake, I hope so. But until then, I just need you to get me my cookies. Do that, and maybe I'll introduce you to some hot friends of Stefano's so you can fall in *L-O-V-E* love. You can have your wedding here next year. We can make an annual Mediterranean trip a thing."

The girl was a hopeless romantic. Why wouldn't she be? She'd found her own Prince Charming, complete with an alpine chalet.

Olivia hugged her best friend to her side. "Don't hold your breath. But before you set me up with a Euro stud, you need me to convince Céline to do a cookie table? You want me to channel an insistent, won't-take-no-for-an-answer New York attitude?"

"Yes." She smiled. "You go and be rude to Céline, so I don't have to be a bridezilla."

"Do I have to be rude right now, though?" Olivia wheedled. "I'm better at getting stuff done when I'm not exhausted."

"I know, babe," Maggie said. "But tomorrow is Céline's day off. The wedding is only a few days away, so I won't have my cookies if I don't get this nailed down. I need you to be on it."

Olivia made a face at her. "Got it. You're the bride. Point me in the right direction."

Mustard stains and all, Olivia marched off to deal with Céline. Sleep would have to wait.

Half an hour later, though, stuck in the hotel underbelly, Olivia was ready to topple over. The sophisticated wedding planner had apparently left her to rot. After graciously professing to understand the cookie table request, Céline explained that she would need to convey the information to the pastry chef. His station was deep inside the kitchen. Olivia was not permitted into that inner sanctum of sweetness, so she waited. And waited.

As Céline's absence stretched past fifteen minutes into infinity, Olivia wasn't sure if the woman was trying to outlast her fading ability to stay awake or if the pastry chef was just incredibly long-winded in his refusal to bake cookies.

After a couple of jarring, jerky head bobs toward oblivion, Olivia reached the desperate stage of exhaustion.

Finally, she heard a door opening and a group of people making their way down the hall. If the elusive Céline wasn't with them, perhaps one of the approaching employees would have access to the kitchen and could take a message.

Olivia careened out the office door and abruptly collided with someone who was definitely not the wedding coordinator.

Nikos Leonikaros jammed his sunglasses over his face and strode briskly out of the paddock team center. He ignored the spectators who yelled across the barrier, begging for his attention. Anyone appearing at the circuit a full week before the race bordered on obsessive. He didn't want to encourage that kind of fan fixation.

He slid into the back seat of the waiting courtesy car. Along with the driver, his security agent, Aleko, was in the front seat. The older man had been with Nikos his entire life, first to protect against kidnapping and ransom, now mostly to keep Nikos's frustrations at bay.

Bryson, Nikos's media director and sometime assistant, also huddled in the back seat, swiping across his ever-present iPad. He'd only been a part of the entourage for a few years. He regularly added to Nikos's frustrations.

"What's on for the rest of the day?" Nikos asked.

"Your lunch should be in the suite when we return to the hotel. Then, you've got an initial strategy and telemetry debrief this afternoon. A workout in the pool. You've got a massage before dinner. Dinner is with TAG Heuer in their hospitality suite—they want to discuss a limited-edition watch. And you've got a lifestyle shoot tonight with them, too. They want some photos by the harbor and some with the car in front of the casino. Clothes for the shoot will be sent up to your room. Pick what you like. We'll bring the rest along in case they want to switch it up."

"And tomorrow…" Nikos said resignedly.

His assistant paused. "Other than your morning workout, you've actually got a free day."

Nikos was stunned.

"Damn."

"I was thinking..." Bryson began.

"Don't think," Nikos interrupted. "You just said it was a free day."

"I know, but we are behind on social content creation."

Nikos groaned. "You know I despise social media."

"It makes the sponsors happy. And it brings new fans to Formula 1."

Nikos glared at him. "Winning races brings new fans to F1. I've been winning since I was seventeen years old. I'm a driver. Not an influencer."

"Well, you can complain all you like," Bryson insisted, "but it's in your contract. And right now, we are behind on the amount of content you're supposed to produce. I thought we could use tomorrow to catch up."

There was no point arguing.

"What do I have to do?" Nikos sighed.

Bryson swiped across the iPad. "The latest concept focuses on drivers' favorite foods. They want to get video of everyone baking their favorite desserts from childhood. There is a kitchen setup at catering we can use, or given that the yacht is here in Monaco, we could get footage in the galley. Give people an exclusive glimpse into the private life of Nikos Leonikaros. They love that."

"No one needs to see inside my yacht or any other aspect of my private life. You know how I feel about that. And a baker? Really? That's perfect," Nikos said sarcastically. "You want a video of me baking cookies I don't eat during the season. *Kourabiedes* aren't exactly on the prescribed diet."

"You just need to make them. Not eat them. And one cookie won't kill you," Bryson retorted. "They want the recipe, too."

Resistance was futile. Nikos shut his eyes.

"I'll call my grandmother for the recipe." He sighed. "So tomorrow, I'm going to be an influencer. And a baker. On my day off."

It never failed to amaze Nikos how his life was no longer his own. Money—even the billions he and his family were worth—didn't buy autonomy. And with fame came confinement.

It hadn't mattered when he was young and living in a glorious bubble. Back then, wealth made it possible to start go-kart racing at the age of five. When he showed some aptitude for motorsports, the money helped him advance. His family could afford the best equipment, training, and travel. And then, when he began to build an enviable record as a driver, his growing fame helped him establish an independent identity from the Leonikaros name. He wasn't merely the son of a Greek shipping magnate but successful in his own right. It was perfect—until wealth and fame sabotaged his relationship with the first girl he'd ever loved and overshadowed every relationship since. As an unintentional celebrity, he had built a life he could barely call his own.

He wasn't sure exactly when, but even some of his joy in racing had dwindled. The heart-stopping thrill of pushing his body and car to unprecedented limits was too often eclipsed by the nonstop demands off track. Everyone wanted a piece of him. Unless he was driving the car, riding his motorcycle, or sailing the boat, he was constantly subject to someone else's agenda.

So, after a lifetime in motorsports, he needed a first-place podium one more time at Monaco to secure the record for most wins on that circuit and then finish the remainder of the season with another world championship. Retirement loomed at the ripe old age of twenty-seven.

The problem was that he had no idea what he was going to do next.

"Service entrance?" The driver asked as they turned onto Avenue des Spélugues.

"Yes," Nikos confirmed before Bryson could say otherwise.

There were drivers for whom being a celebrity was still a thrilling novelty. They would walk through the Hôtel de Paris front door and bask in the adulation of the admirers haunting the entrance and lobby. But because of the threats his father's wealth attracted, Nikos had been raised to be cautious in public. He always used back entrances and went incognito when and where he could. Now he wondered if true anonymity would ever be possible, if he could escape the frustrations of a lifestyle he'd never meant to pursue.

Aleko scanned the area and opened the car door

for Nikos. The hotel security guard quickly waved them into the building.

Nikos removed his sunglasses and followed Aleko through the labyrinth of service corridors. Bryson strode ahead, still swiping. Nikos glanced down at his watch and eagerly anticipated taking the private elevator to his suite to enjoy his midday meal alone, free of his minders for at least a few hours. Maybe he could watch a movie.

Before he realized what was happening, a blur of motion sprang at him, bursting into the corridor from behind a partially closed office door. Nikos had quick reflexes and was nimble enough to avoid being knocked against the opposite wall, but only by catching hold of the human cannonball.

Bryson yelped; Aleko swung around, poised to neutralize any threat. The situation teetered on the edge of chaos.

Except there wasn't a threat. She wasn't a threat. Nikos wasn't sure how he knew, but there was no doubt in his mind that the lovely but rumpled girl staring up at him wide-eyed meant no harm.

Curiously, there wasn't a hint of recognition in her hazel eyes. She appeared to have no idea she'd nearly taken down the number one driver in the world.

"Oh my God, I am so sorry!"

She was American by her accent. That might explain it. The US fan base for Formula 1 racing was small but growing. Perhaps she didn't know who he was. That was a novelty.

She continued to hold fast to Nikos's forearms as he held hers. He tried to shift her to one side to step around, but she simultaneously shifted in the same direction. Once again, in an awkward parody of a dance, they bumped against one another, arms still clasped.

"Sorry—oh whoops—sorry…sorry," she apologized.

Nikos was used to having women throw themselves at him, dropping hints and shedding clothing. There had been women who had tried to accost him, sneaking into hotel suites, reserved paddock areas, and VIP enclosures in restaurants. He'd managed to dodge them all. Or at least the ones he wanted to dodge. This woman, however, had succeeded in blindsiding him, literally and figuratively.

She appeared genuinely mortified by their collision. Yet despite her discombobulated state, there was something appealing about her, coupled with an inexplicable sense of déjà vu. His body was humming. Was it the endorphins from his earlier workout? Or perhaps it was just the weird buzz of fluorescent lighting? The whole exchange was bizarre.

He was intrigued, to say the least.

Gently, almost unwillingly, he disentangled himself from her grasp, and she held up her palms apologetically.

"Again, I am so sorry. I just got to Monaco. I've

been awake for thirty-six hours and am completely loopy."

Somehow, he didn't think she was here for the race.

"It's all right—it was an accident. No harm done."

She swiped her hand over her head, her fingers lifting her hair from the roots. The silken strands slid through her fingers, and he envisioned her illuminated by ocean sunlight, like a goddess risen from the sea.

The image took his breath away. Damn. Who was this girl? And why was he unable to look away? No one had caught his attention like this since... well, in a very long time.

In that instant, the exhilaration of anonymity was profound. Until this chance encounter, Nikos hadn't realized how badly he wanted someone to look at him like this girl was looking at him. To not presume any knowledge, but to see him as a stranger to discover. And to allow him the opportunity to discover her in return. Someone who would see him as Nikos—not Nikos Leonikaros, celebrity F1 driver—just Nikos.

Visceral desire flooded his senses.

He held his breath. She looked him over quizzically. Calculating. "Could I ask you a favor?"

The bubble burst; his heart sank. He knew that look. He knew it from every autograph seeker, his conniving ex-girlfriend, Athena, and every woman he'd since dated. They all wanted him primarily for his celebrity status and its benefits.

Despite this girl's initial innocent expression, she, too, had apparently recognized him and she wanted something. It was inescapable. No wonder he was suspicious of every person he met. No wonder he was ready to retire. Until he quit racing and stepped out of the public eye, the kind of connection he craved would remain elusive.

The sizzling flare of attraction had gone cold. He needed to wrap it up.

"Sure. What do you want?"

Bryson stepped up and held out a Sharpie for the anticipated autograph request.

She regarded Bryson perplexedly, then turned back to Nikos.

"I'm trying to find Céline, the wedding coordinator, and she disappeared into the kitchen about twenty minutes ago." She pointed to the stainless-steel door across the corridor. "I need someone who works here to take a message to her and tell her to forget it. I can't wait any longer… I'm going to pass out from exhaustion."

"Take a message?"

Hope surged back through his body. Nikos bit the insides of his cheeks to keep the hilarious disbelief from showing. Did this girl really think he was staff at the hotel?

"Are you maybe kitchen or hospitality? Front desk?"

Nikos couldn't help it; he gave her a wry grin. Bryson's jaw dropped. Aleko's eyes widened.

Nikos quirked an intentional eyebrow at his assistant and then somberly addressed the girl: "I'm a baker."

If she had surprised him by barreling into him, now her reaction astonished him.

"A baker?!" She gasped with all the enthusiasm of a rabid racing fan. "Are you kidding me? You are just who I need to talk to!"

"I am?"

"Yes." She exhaled dramatically. "Oh, this is perfect. Oh my God. Okay. My friend is getting married at the hotel and needs someone to bake. She needs American cookies, not French pastries."

"I'm Greek," he offered.

"Perfect!" She lifted her hands and gazed upward in emphasis. "Greeks own just about every diner in New York. And I've had some amazing cookies in those diners. You get what I'm trying to say. You understand what I need."

Nikos was speechless. Aleko looked like he might pass out. Bryson was fighting not to laugh.

"So you need cookies?"

"Yes." She glanced side to side as if she feared being overheard. "And no offense, I don't think the French pastry chef at the hotel is the right person to bake them."

"Definitely not," Nikos agreed. He had no idea how long he could keep up the farce, but he was willing to string it along indefinitely. This was the most entertainment he'd had in ages. And a persistent voice inside his head suggested that engaging with this captivating girl might be an extraordinary opportunity to discover what a woman might see in him beyond his money and fame.

"So what do you recommend? Can you bake the cookies in the hotel kitchen even if the pastry chef won't? Or would that be frowned upon?" She hesitated. "That is, I should first ask if you are willing to help me. Are you? I wouldn't want to get you in trouble."

"How about this…" Nikos was thinking fast. He typically spent some of his off-season in Monte Carlo. He knew the shops and the restaurants. If they went out early, before the city awoke and the streets got crowded…

"I can't bake cookies here at the hotel. So how about I take you around to all the pâtisseries early tomorrow? I know the city. I'm sure we can find someone who can bake the cookies you want."

He wasn't ready to invite her onto the yacht and have his staff bake whatever she needed. He wasn't crazy. And it would require too much of an explanation. He'd have to correct her misperceptions about who he was. But if the morning went well…

"Oh my God." Her eyes softened. "Thank you so much—that would be amazing. But…" She frowned. "How are we going to get around town? Just getting to the hotel was a nightmare. I guess there's a race coming up. They've got streets blocked for the course and grandstands."

Nikos swallowed a laugh.

"A race," he repeated. "Yes. A Grand Prix. You're not a racing fan, huh?"

She shrugged. "No. I'm not much of a sports fan in general. I'll go to a baseball game, but that's more for the vibes."

"I've never been to a baseball game. But Formula 1 racing has a lot of vibes," he suggested.

"I'm sure it does. I just have no particular interest."

A look of horrified comprehension washed over her face. "Oh, I see your shirt. I'm so sorry. I bet you're a big fan. I'm not trying to be rude. I'm sure it's a really cool sport. A great time. No offense."

"None taken." He smiled. "But back to your cookies. I've got a bike. We can get around the barricades."

"A bike, huh?" She tilted her head. She paused and scrutinized him. He couldn't blame her; she'd just been invited to accompany a total stranger around a foreign city. Did she have a sense of adventure?

Say yes, say yes, his heart thudded.

"Is this a bike, as in a vehicle you pedal? Or is it a Vespa? Or a motorcycle? What are we talking about?"

Fluttery, flirtatious bubbles rose in his chest.

He could get any kind of bike she liked, although he desperately wanted her on the back of his Ducati. Unbidden, he imagined her arms encircling his body…

She blushed as if she could read his thoughts. Or was she having similar thoughts of her own? Either way, she didn't appear to be put off, which was encouraging. But he still wasn't sure she would accept. There was uncertainty, and he wasn't used to uncertainty with women. This was a challenge. He liked challenges.

God, say yes.

"What kind of bike would you prefer?"

She grinned flirtatiously at him. "Oh, no you don't. I'm already exhausted and babbling, so don't ask me what I prefer. Just tell me what kind of bike to expect. I'm game."

He cracked an unfiltered grin. "Expect to have to hang on tight. It's a motorcycle. I'll meet you in the alley outside the back door at eight o'clock. The exit is down this corridor and to the right. Does that work?"

She bit her lip, looking adorably pleased, and nodded.

"Okay, then I'll see you tomorrow..." She laughed and ducked past Bryson and Aleko with a little wave.

Just as she was about to disappear around the corner into the next corridor, Nikos called out. "Hey!"

She twisted back toward him. He could see her cheeks flush even from a distance.

"What's your name?"

"Liv. Olivia. What's yours?"

"Nikos. Just Nikos."

MONDAY MORNING

OLIVIA STRETCHED DECADENTLY in the crisp white sheets and sighed with contentment. There was nothing better than waking up in a hotel bed, especially in such an exquisite, golden-hued room. She'd crashed hard the day before, forgetting to close the drapes in her single-minded focus on sleep. Now she was bathed in early-morning light, illuminating her room and the palm-fringed, crystalline harbor below. Yachts of every conceivable configuration bobbed in tidy rows. Buildings, tinged pink in sunlight, rose in layers against the cliffs. The scenery was utterly unreal.

A knock interrupted her reverie.

She padded to the door and peeked out. Mags, accompanied by a hotel employee, stood in the hall.

"Good morning, sunshine! Room service!" Maggie exclaimed as Olivia opened the door. Mags handed the attendant a few euros after the food trolley had been discreetly positioned.

"May I tempt you?" Maggie lifted the corner of a linen napkin to reveal a pile of pastries in a sterling-silver basket.

"Oh yes, please."

Olivia debated the impossible choice between a croissant and a *pain au chocolat*. She decided there could be no wrong selection. She chose the latter and groaned as the flaky dough and rich chocolate melted in her mouth.

"Yeah, I can see why you wouldn't want anything like this at your wedding. This totally sucks." She took another emphatic bite.

"Shut up." Maggie grinned as she poured coffee into two porcelain cups. "So? I got your text yesterday about Plan B for Operation Cookie Table. Do tell."

"Okay..." Olivia finished the last scrumptious bite and washed it down with a swallow of fresh-squeezed orange juice. "I lost track of Céline, but I arranged a date with a Greek baker who works here at the hotel to visit every pastry shop in Monte Carlo this morning."

The look on Maggie's face was priceless. *"What?"*

Olivia started laughing and nearly choked on her first bite of croissant. "I know, right?"

"Damn, girl. You move fast. Say more."

"So, I ran into him...literally ran into him...in the corridor outside Céline's office. We got to talking..."

"Talking?" Maggie rolled her eyes.

"Yes. Maggie, I wasn't flirting. My focus was entirely on your need for cookies. Not how scrumptiously good-looking this guy was. I didn't even notice."

"Right. All cookie business. Tell me more about this guy. He's totally hot?"

Olivia raised an eyebrow in wicked confirmation. "Why, yes. Yes, he is. I don't even know how to describe it. There was…is…something about him. He isn't a very big guy. Not super tall. But he has an incredibly fit body. Not bulging muscles. Really lithe and lean. Like, not an ounce of fat."

"How would you know his fat ratio? I mean, the man was presumably wearing clothes, right?" Maggie demanded.

"I told you I physically ran into him. And then we did that awkward thing where you bump into someone, then you both go the same way and bump again."

"Two bumps and you could tell everything you needed to know?"

"Absolutely," Olivia insisted. "And it wasn't just his body…" She gave Maggie an arched look. "He has really striking green-blue eyes. And silky, sun-kissed brown hair. It's short in the back but flops over his face in the front. It makes him look kind of shy."

"Shy? He asked you on a date after two bumps. That's not shy."

Olivia grinned and shrugged. "The sacrifices I make for you. If I have to hang on to the back of a hot guy on a motorcycle to make your wedding dreams come true, I'll do it…"

"A motorcycle!" Maggie squealed. But then she frowned. "What are you going to wear? Did your suitcase arrive?"

Olivia pushed up off the bed. "No, not yet. I thought about it. I have a plan." She rummaged through her backpack and pulled out her carefully rolled pajamas. "I slept in my sweats, but I have these—they're new linen drawstring pajamas with a cropped shirt. I bought the set to double as a bathing suit cover-up if I needed one. So, these over my bikini…" She pulled out the bathing suit and dangled it for Maggie's assessment. "I thought it would be a good boho look."

"I like it," Maggie affirmed. "But you need some accessories. Come to my room, and we'll see what works. I've got a Prada mini crossbody you can use. And I bought you gold metallic Birkenstock sandals to say thanks for being my maid of honor and making this trip. Oh!"

"What?"

"I've got some vintage silk scarves from Stefano's mom. I think one is Hermès and the other is Pucci. I tie them onto my purses. But if you are going to be on a motorcycle, you could wear one tied over your hair."

"Like a bandana?"

"No, more like a fortune teller, if you know what I mean?"

Olivia cackled, waiving her hands over the coffee pot like a crystal ball. "In my future, I see a handsome blue-eyed stranger who tastes suspiciously like Greek sugar cookies…"

"Tastes?" Maggie hooted. "That escalated quickly. Behave, Madame Boho, or you will have a hundred years of bad luck. Or not. Maybe you'll have a hot Greek for lunch."

Olivia batted her eyes and mocked her friend primly. "Thank you, Margaret. Without you and your bridezilla demands, I wouldn't have a date with Nikos."

"Nikos, Nikos—hot, hot Nikos," Mags chanted in a sing-song accent. Olivia threw a pillow at her.

"I just hope he's not an exhaustion-induced fever dream…" Olivia admitted.

A half hour later, in the golden morning light, she watched Nikos take off his helmet and run his hand through his hair, the beads of his bracelets sliding along his wrist. Fitted white T-shirt. Faded jeans. Eyes as brilliant as the Mediterranean. He was no fever dream. He was gorgeously, gloriously real. A travel fling on her whirlwind trip to Monaco hadn't been on the itinerary; however, since the possibility so attractively presented itself and facilitated her bridesmaid responsibilities, who was she to refuse?

Grinning like a fool, she walked toward him. She knew that she was rocking her improvised outfit. Mags had done her makeup, giving Olivia a natural-looking glow. She was a far cry from the bedraggled waif she'd been the day before.

Olivia projected confidence, but inside, she acknowledged a certain amount of false bravado and tempered expectations. She had no idea who this guy was or what they were about to do. And no matter how strongly she was attracted to him—and holy moly, she was attracted to him—she was heading back to New York in five days. But perhaps a sizzling holiday romance was exactly what she needed. It wouldn't—couldn't—go anywhere, but damn, a Monte Carlo adventure with a hot guy might be the perfect morale boost before diving back into the eternally disappointing New York dating scene.

Nikos remained still, eyeing her approach. He wasn't blatantly gawping; he wasn't leering. But a subtle expression of pleasure passed over his face. The appreciative look warmed Olivia to the core, and she strolled with a bit more sway. Her bravado shifted into actual confidence. Whatever she was doing with Nikos, it felt inexplicably right.

"Good morning, Nikos," she called out.

"*Kaliméra*, Olivia."

She grinned. She didn't speak Greek, but the sentiment was clear. "I wasn't sure if you were going to show up. I thought I might have dreamed our whole conversation."

"But here I am," he replied. He flashed an endearing, sexy smile. He was pleased to see her, perhaps even eager. There was nothing cocky about him, which was surprising given the sleek beast of a motorcycle he straddled.

The bike looked fast. Really fast. And dangerous.

Olivia should have been terrified at the thought of zooming through an unfamiliar city, hanging precariously on the back of a total stranger. Yet the butterflies in her stomach weren't from fear. Instead, she was almost giddy, as though embarking on a journey to some previously unknown but incredibly desirable destination.

Even so, she had to ask.

"Can you handle this bike with someone riding behind? Tell me the truth. Are you a good driver?"

He looked at her, perplexedly, like she had two heads, as if the answer was a foregone conclusion. Sure, it had been a silly question, a way to buy time before she fully committed to getting on the motorcycle. There was no way he would admit to being a lousy driver, even if he were. No guy would acknowledge that kind of shortcoming.

"I can handle the bike," he insisted.

"Look, it's just that I've never ridden a motorcycle before. By myself or with anyone else," she admitted.

"It's easy," he said. "You just have to hang on and let me do the rest."

"I can do that," she agreed. "I think."

He had an extra helmet attached to the back of the bike. He twisted his torso in a beautiful, fluid motion and unfastened the spare.

"Come here," he beckoned.

The sultry, quiet demand set Olivia's heart pounding. The butterflies in her stomach morphed into happy, back-flipping otters. Hoping she looked calmer than she felt, she moved closer, close enough to smell the spice of his cologne, mingled with the burnt scent of the bike's engine. It was an intoxicating combination. Oh yeah, she would enjoy getting to know him better.

"Lean forward. Let me help you with this."

With a deep breath, she complied. He settled the spare helmet on her head.

His attentiveness was surprisingly lovely. She'd never wanted or allowed a man to fuss over her, but she had to admit that the kindness in the simple gesture of helping with her helmet was appealing.

"Good idea to wear a scarf over your hair," he muttered while he adjusted the chin strap.

It was odd, Olivia thought. He was a stranger, yet he'd touched her both times they'd been face-to-face, and it felt perfectly natural. Yesterday he had clutched her to keep from falling, and now his fingers brushed against the sensitive skin where her neck met her jaw.

In each instance, his touch had been innocent. Usually, if a guy put his hand on her, no matter how casually, it was a precursor to something sexual. Which was fine—everybody knew the game. Except that Nikos's gentle, considerate contact somehow made her feel cared for, tended to, in a strange and unprecedented way that was even more irresistible.

"Okay." He nodded, satisfied with the helmet's fit. "Your seat is probably going to be a little uncomfortable. I hadn't planned to use this bike to ride with anyone else. This model is more for racing than a touring bike. It's not really designed for someone to ride pillion. In fact, I was going to remove the passenger pegs—I didn't think I'd need them. I just haven't gotten around to it."

He paused abruptly, and she realized she wasn't the only one prone to babbling. Despite his confident assurance that he could handle the bike, she wondered if he, too, might feel some eager butterflies at the prospect of their outing together. She smiled through the helmet's visor. He grinned back.

"Here, can you get on behind?"

He steadied himself so she might take hold of his shoulder. She clutched him and felt a little thrill at the bones and sinews in her grasp. She kicked her leg up over the bike and shifted onto it. The seat pitched her at an angle toward his body. He twisted back to look at her, and she nearly banged his face with her helmet.

"Hold on to me," he instructed. "Put both your feet up on the pegs. You'll feel more balanced, and it will be easier once we're moving."

In following his instructions, she tipped even further forward against his back. She placed her hands on his waist, trying to create space between their bodies and to position herself with some decorum. After all, no matter how tempting, it felt supremely bizarre to wrap her arms around someone she'd just met. He reached for his helmet. Touching him, she was hyperaware of the stretch and pull of his muscles moving under his T-shirt. She tried not to think about the sensation of her inner thighs squeezing against him.

He leaned forward. "Ready?"

"Uh-huh." She gulped.

He flicked something, and the bike roared to life. Olivia panicked at the sudden power and unexpected thrust. Decorum be damned, she plastered herself to his torso and wrapped her arms around him tight as a Band-Aid. But slowly, as she acclimated to their forward movement, she began to breathe and slightly loosened her grip. She opened her eyes to make sense of the world blurring by in an incomprehensible rush. For a fleeting moment, she thought she might get the hang of riding pillion.

Suddenly, Nikos leaned low and sideways, pulling the bike and their bodies almost parallel to the ground. They swung around a corner. Terrified, Olivia squashed tightly against him once more, anticipating imminent death. Then, Nikos straightened back up, and they swung in the opposite direction. And back. Again and again through the twisting streets. It was too much.

Riding pillion was like the roiling sensation of being on a carnival ride that had been allowed to run too fast and for too long. She wanted the ride to end but feared it would end badly. Painfully. She dizzily squeezed her eyes shut and fervently prayed to any friendly deity who might be sympathetic to the pleas of a girl so easily enticed by an attractive man on a bike. The gods just laughed. The motorcycle thundered on.

No sooner had she surrendered all hope of survival than the bike growled to a stop, the engine cut, and Nikos dropped his legs. Olivia was too paralyzed to move.

"You can let go now," he hinted. "We're here. Rue Grimaldi."

Shaking, Olivia peeled her arms from his warm body. Clutching his shoulders, she placed one foot on terra firma and awkwardly hauled her leg over the bike.

With trembling fingers, she unfastened the now claustrophobic helmet and tugged it off.

He turned to her, his face unreadable behind his tinted visor. "Too much?" he asked.

"Um, no, yeah. Wow. Yeah. Give me a minute."

She sensed he was laughing—actually laughing. Was he nuts? Was she the only one who felt like they had cheated death a thousand times in under ten minutes?

"Sorry." He shrugged with a chuckle. "I tried to take it easy."

"Oh, my dear God," she muttered. "That was taking it easy? I can't even..."

"Anyhow," he continued while she attempted to breathe normally. "The first pâtisserie is across the street. There isn't any place to park, so I'll circle around while you talk to them about the cookies. I'll be back to pick you up." He paused and cocked his head. "That is, if you want me to come back for you?"

She steeled herself and shook off her jitters. As unbelievable as it was…they had survived.

"Despite my deeply held conviction that you nearly killed me, um, yeah…" she said shakily. "Please do come back for me. Thanks."

He nodded. She crossed the street on unsteady legs. She heard the roar of the bike as he sped off.

Now it was time to do her assigned job and focus on procuring cookies. She needed to ignore the whiff of his cologne still clinging to her linen shirt. Focus. She needed to focus.

But she had no luck in the pastry shop. Everything looked mouth-wateringly delicious, and the woman behind the counter was exceedingly polite. But before Olivia could describe exactly what she needed, the woman apologetically explained that they were at capacity for special orders because of the upcoming Grand Prix. Apparently, lots of fans meant a high demand for baked goods. It made sense, but it was discouraging.

Olivia crossed to where Nikos had returned, the bike's engine still running.

"No." She shook her head. "They can't do it."

"That was just the first shop," he said reassuringly. "I'm sure we can find what you need somewhere else. We can keep going."

Once again, he helped her with her helmet while she mentally repeated the old adage about getting back in the saddle. Of course, the saying referred to a horse, not a bike capable of breaking the sound barrier. She inhaled a deep breath for courage and flung herself onto the bike. Had she lost her mind? It was a distinct possibility.

Like a python, she twined her arms around Nikos and propped her feet onto the pegs. As they sped off, before fear and adrenaline consumed her, Olivia realized she'd wrapped herself around him without a second thought. It was as if holding him close was the most natural thing in the world. As they leaned into another turn, she wondered how it would feel to be so intimate if they weren't riding a two-wheeled rocket. Holding him, she concluded, was very, very appealing. If they survived their motorcycle adventure, she definitely wanted to get close to him when they were on steady, unmoving ground.

Over the following hours, they visited countless other pastry shops, each with a similar response: *Sorry, not sorry, we can't help you this week. All special orders are for Grand Prix parties.*

It was frustrating.

Nikos patiently suggested each successive stop—after all, Olivia had no idea how many pastry shops were in Monte Carlo—but she noticed a subtle transformation in him as the sun rose higher and the streets became more crowded. His words were polite, but his tone grew terse. And because of their forced proximity, she could feel the increasing tension in his body.

After another negative response from a pastry shop in a particularly crowded area, she had barely settled onto the bike before he shot off, weaving precariously through throngs of people, some of whom stopped and stared.

Once loose and fluid, his body now felt like he'd been wrapped in steel coils, emanating stress. Clearly, he was losing patience. Whether with her or with the errand…she wasn't sure, but she didn't want to continue if he was unwilling and reckless. She'd spent her childhood hyperaware of her father's body language, learning to recognize any pending eruption. She knew what male frustration looked like.

"Hey!" she yelled and poked him as they accelerated to an alarming speed on a long straightaway. He abruptly banked into a turn, and they halted in a deserted alleyway.

"I don't think this is going to work, and I don't want to take up any more of your time," she blurted over the still-loud engine.

She felt his body sag in apparent relief.

Okay, she thought. It was fun while it lasted. Who knew traveling at death-defying speeds could be enjoyable? Hanging on to a ridiculously attractive guy wasn't the worst way to have spent the morning. The outing wasn't a total loss.

He cut the engine so they could speak at a normal volume.

"I apologize. I feel awful. I truly thought this would be easy," he said with obvious frustration.

Was that it? Was Nikos a man who became irritable at any perceived challenge or, God forbid, failure? She'd known plenty of guys like that, starting with her father. He had been one for grand dramatic gestures…so long as they suited his purposes or fed his ego. But when complications arose or it was no longer convenient for him to accommodate a wife or a daughter, he'd lie, make excuses, or punish them for his failures, withholding affection and financial support. So, she'd learned to take care of herself, thank you very much. She had no tolerance for men who got angry at the first sign of complication, men who twisted the narrative to bolster their own self-image.

"It's not your fault." She sighed. "We can head back to the hotel. Thank you. I appreciate the effort."

Which was true. But she wouldn't stroke his ego and gush about how wonderful he was just for trying, even though his offer to help had been rather remarkable. When they'd started out that morning, she'd been intrigued and enticed by his seemingly selfless act. What guy gave up his morning for a stranger? But if he couldn't handle a less-than-optimal outcome without getting upset, she had no further interest.

Unfortunately, it also meant that Olivia might as well accept that she wouldn't be able to provide the one thing her best friend wanted, something money alone couldn't buy, something that celebrated their shared history.

Nikos paused before firing up the bike again. He looked like he was about to speak. Olivia waited for the inevitable defensiveness.

"Would you want to get lunch?"

The question took her by surprise. Was it possible that Nikos wasn't bothered by the morning's failure? Was he able to simply move on without pouting? That was unusual for a guy.

A renewed tingling of curiosity and attraction replaced her skepticism.

Nikos had offered to help the American girl on a wild whim. He was rarely spontaneous, but the novelty of being unrecognized had been too appealing to refuse. Nor could he deny Olivia's inexplicable allure.

He had expected a brief but amusing outing. Afterward, he assumed he'd return her to the hotel and spend his afternoon at the gym.

But as the morning progressed, after each disappointing stop, she'd gamely climbed back onto the bike despite her obvious nervousness. She'd twined her arms trustingly around his waist. And no matter what his rational mind cautioned, his body thrilled to her touch. But more than his blatant physical response, their time together piqued a long-suppressed desire for genuine connection. He'd felt it the first moment they'd met.

He had time to think as he circled Monte Carlo, waiting for her to emerge from each shop. He decided it was worth skipping his workout to enjoy her company a little longer.

But why? What exactly were they doing? Had their excursion morphed into a date? Was that what he wanted all along? Ever since the explosive breakup with Athena that almost derailed his career ten years earlier, Nikos had largely avoided dating during the season. And when he did date…

There were objectively stunning women in his past. Finding a woman to appreciate the fit body he spent so much time cultivating was easy. And sex with a gorgeous woman was, theoretically, more entertaining than watching movies, playing video games, or playing padel. And yet…these increasingly infrequent encounters left him dissatisfied. He felt no emotional involvement, depth, or passion with anyone he dated. And he was sick of being nothing more than passing entertainment, a means of bolstering a woman's status, or a way for her to access the perks of wealth and fame. Yes, everyone understood the game and what was being bartered and traded. It was purely transactional. Nothing more. Lately, the effort of dating simply wasn't worth it.

Today, however, he reveled in the unprecedented opportunity to slip his tiresome identity and experience the enchantment of a mysterious woman who knew as little about him as he knew of her.

It was incredibly freeing. It threw him back to being an anonymous sixteen-year-old consumed with the angst and ecstasy of his first real crush, when he'd first met Athena, before they were caught up in fame and all its temptations. Before Athena sacrificed his heart to the altar of her own greed and ego. Before she'd cheated on him while burning through an obscene percentage of his early winnings. After their breakup, he'd sworn never to let anyone get close enough to eviscerate him again. He had easily kept that vow.

But now his surprising attraction to this girl triggered an intoxication and foolhardy rush he'd not felt in a long time. Her sense of adventure and loyalty to her friend intrigued him.

He didn't want their adventure to end, but unfortunately, the likelihood of being recognized had increased every time they stopped. So, while Olivia visited yet another pâtisserie, Nikos optimistically contacted Bryson to reserve the discreet terrace at his favorite café. For a price, they'd cordon off the entire space. Nikos and Olivia could slip in the back. He made it clear that no one was to hint at his identity. He needed to explore the freedom of anonymity a little longer. He refused to risk the crushing disappointment of seeing greed take the place of curiosity in the eyes of a girl who appeared to be as attracted to him as he was to her. Perhaps their fledgling connection might increase over the intimacy of a meal together. He desperately wanted to find out.

When Olivia suggested they give up on the cookie quest, Nikos twisted around to gauge her mood. Hopefully, her obvious irritation wasn't directed at him. Was she too annoyed to accept an invitation to continue their day together?

"Would you want to get lunch?"

He could tell he had surprised her. Nikos's stomach dropped at the thought of being refused. The last time he worried about being turned down was a decade earlier, before he'd gotten behind the wheel of an F1 car. But more importantly, he wasn't used to caring that a woman might reject him.

"Sure, that would be great."

Inordinately pleased, he fired up the bike and reminded himself to take it at a reasonable pace, no matter how eager he was to go somewhere to get to know her better.

At the café, they were seated in a tranquil garden bordered with clay pots of fresh herbs—rosemary, mint, and thyme. Their mingled scent reminded Nikos of home, his parents contentedly puttering about on the patio with a view of the sea, tending their fragrant plants. He'd always assumed he might do the same with his wife someday. Based on his grandparents' and parents' loving marriages, he'd taken it for granted that he would find a woman with whom he could build a family, share a home, and enjoy life's simple pleasures. But that assumption had shattered with Athena, and he'd found no one with whom to resurrect that dream. But now he couldn't quash the tiny but defiant spark that wondered if the girl sitting across from him might represent that possibility.

"It's strange that no one else is here," Olivia commented. "It's such a gorgeous day."

Nikos shrugged. "I think this café gets crowded for dinner."

Olivia eyed the menu, periodically glancing at him with subtle but encouraging scrutiny.

The server kept his gaze averted, granting Nikos the anonymity he'd paid for.

"Une bouteille d'eau, s'il vous plait..." Nikos requested. He might've been willing to skip the gym, but he didn't want to go so far as to order wine. He hoped Olivia wouldn't find that odd.

"...plate ou gazeuse?" the server replied.

Before he could respond, Olivia answered confidently in passable French that she preferred sparkling water.

Interesting.

She was American but had possibly spent some time in Europe. His curiosity piqued.

"We don't know each other, but I think I would like to get to know you, Olivia… Olivia… Olivia…?" Nikos realized a critical gap in his knowledge.

"Keller?" she prompted helpfully.

He grinned and tried it out, "Olivia Keller."

"What do you want to know about me, Nikos… Nikos…?" she mimicked.

"Nikolaes Giorgos Alexandros Christos Michális Leonikaros." The syllables rolled off his tongue at lightning speed. Hopefully, she'd not extract *Nikos Leonikaros*, much less associate the name with an F1 driver.

"I'm afraid I got lost in that mouthful," she teased. "I'm going to need you to repeat your name one more time for me. And maybe spell it out."

"Not a chance." He shook his head. "Just stick with Nikos."

"Okay, just Nikos. You can call me Liv. What do you want to know about me?"

"You are American. What part of the US are you from?"

"I currently work in New York City but grew up in Pittsburgh."

He blanked, so she clarified. "It's in Pennsylvania, which is a big state. Pittsburgh is about eight hours from New York City. Have you ever been to New York?"

"When I was a child," he replied, smiling at the memory. "My family went to New York City. I was young—all I remember is eating a hot dog from a cart on the street. Have you ever been to Greece?"

She shook her head. "No, but I'd love to visit. What part of the country are you from?"

"A tiny island called Kallitheira, in the southern Cyclades. The island has belonged to my family for centuries. I am related to everyone there."

"And I thought New York was a tough dating pool. It's got to be rough trying to find a girlfriend on a family island," she joked.

She was fishing for information about his relationship status. So maybe this was a date? His heart gave a happy thump.

"It is tough. I had no choice but to come to Monte Carlo to find a beautiful American girl."

She laughed out loud.

"Yikes. That is a pretty cheesy pickup line." She

looked flattered nonetheless. "Do girls in Monaco fall for it?"

How would he know? He'd never tried to pick up a girl in Monaco or anywhere else with a pickup line. He didn't need to.

"Probably not. This is the first time I've said it."

"Well, that's okay, then. I'm susceptible to flattery, especially because you are honest about its effectiveness."

Honest.

He tried not to cringe. If she only knew. She'd probably be appalled if he explained how he met prospective romantic partners.

Nikos and the women he dated had support staff. Publicists contacted assistants, and media managers chatted at celebrity galas. Overtures and introductions were made. VIP areas at clubs and restaurants were secured. Rooms were booked on the same floor of the same hotel. The F1 driver was photographed with the supermodel. Or singer. Or actress. When the season got intense, the pop tour launched, or movie production began, then both parties went their separate ways. What passed for a relationship often played out on social media, which he despised. The whole unappetizing process was soul-wearying and precisely why Nikos wasn't currently dating...and why pickup lines weren't his strong suit.

But facing retirement, perhaps it was time to try a new approach to dating. One that might result in a genuine relationship. For that, he had to get to know her better.

"Tell me about what you do in New York City..."

He couldn't venture a guess.

"The short answer is that I help large multinational corporations with risk assessment."

"Wow." He whistled. "That's quite impressive."

"Tell it to my boss." She shrugged. "Maybe I'll get a raise. What's it like being a baker in Monte Carlo?"

He replied with a noncommittal "meh." He wanted to discourage her from questioning him too closely. His ruse would unravel if she discovered he knew next to nothing about baking.

"So, you are here for a wedding?"

This time, her smile was broad and unfiltered. It dazzled him. What would it be like to be the reason for a smile like that?

"Yes! Until Saturday. My best friend is getting married to a guy from Zurich. She met him when we did a study abroad. Maggie and I have known each other since birth. We're like sisters."

"Do you have other siblings?"

"Nope. Basically, it's just me and my mom." She pursed her lips, clearly unwilling to say more.

Her response was ambiguous, but he didn't think he should push her. It was odd talking to a stranger for whom he had no preconceived idea of their life. Getting to know someone freed from the usual celebrity image and status-related presumptions was fascinating.

"And you? What is your family like?" she turned the conversation.

At least he didn't have to lie. He just needed to be selective about the details.

"Where to begin?" He shook his head in amusement. "There are a lot of us. Not only my two older sisters and parents, but a host of grandparents, aunts, uncles, and cousins. Lots of random spouses and second cousins. And everyone is very lovingly but aggressively in each other's business, all the time."

"And they all live on this island? Together?"

"Mostly, although many of us spend time in different parts of Europe for various reasons. Jobs. School. But home is Kallitheira."

"That sounds incredible." She nodded. "Very insular, so probably intimidating for anyone who visits, but to have that many people in your family to rely on must be really comforting. You're lucky. I bet it's beautiful there."

The accuracy of Olivia's insight knocked the breath out of him. Few comprehended or appreciated the unique dynamics of his family and their home. Certainly Athena hadn't. She'd tolerated his family so that she might access their wealth to cultivate a flashy public image. She'd sensationalized her relationship with Nikos—including her poisonous affair with a rival driver—to titillate an insatiable social media audience. Her obsession with creating a buzz for herself had betrayed everything Nikos's family valued. After their relationship exploded, Nikos had never introduced another woman to his family's distinctive way of life. It was safer to separate his private and public personas.

Now it astounded him that a girl from such a different background could be so astute in her understanding. And talking with someone oblivious to his fame, he could instead share stories of his childhood and the people he loved.

As they ate, he told her about racing bicycles with his cousins on his island's infrequently used airstrip. She responded with tales of the ice rink where she learned how to skate as a child and how she now loved to skate at the iconic rink under the Christmas tree in Rockefeller Plaza. He'd seen the place in movies and could imagine her spinning on the ice, her hair twirling around her face.

Their conversation prompted memories he'd almost forgotten. It was an incredible feeling, and he realized he definitely wanted this unanticipated connection to continue. The girl enthralled him. One more meetup couldn't hurt. But how far should he carry his false identity? Was it worth confessing now? How should he explain it?

Despite an undeniable attraction, he also had to be realistic. During race week, his time wasn't his own. They'd both be gone in a few short days. He didn't want to overcommit. He didn't want to give her the wrong idea, even if he wasn't sure what the wrong idea might be.

So what did he want with Olivia Keller? He

wasn't sure, but fortunately, the cookies were a perfect excuse to see her again.

After their charming lunch, Olivia walked beside Nikos back to his bike. During the meal, he'd never once bragged about himself, as guys were apt to do on first dates. Instead, he'd asked questions about her life and actually listened to what she had to say. It was bizarre. It was appealing.

"I've been thinking about your cookies, and I have a backup plan," Nikos said. "But I need to make some arrangements. Can I get in touch later?"

Olivia hesitated. He sounded sincere, but she simply couldn't wrap her head around a guy who would help her when it didn't benefit him. Hell, her ex-boyfriend Sebastian pitched a fit when she asked him to go around the block to pick up take-out rather than wait on delivery for his own dinner!

And how many false promises had she heard? Her dad had always promised the moon. Countless times he said he'd take her clothes shopping or pay for new skates and lessons. He had insisted he would cover the cost of her tuition. But inevitably, he failed to deliver anything other than pathetic excuses. Olivia and her mom were left scrambling. On those rare occasions when the man did produce some unexpected, extravagant gift or grand gesture, it always came with strings attached. Olivia had learned to always look a gift horse in the mouth.

Seriously, what guy was generous without expecting something in return? What did Nikos want? His offer seemed too complicated to simply be a ploy to hook up. Which, in all honesty, she might agree to regardless. Was he just an incredibly thoughtful guy?

She couldn't fathom it, but perhaps she was too quick to assume the worst. And she still needed cookies. The clock was ticking. If Nikos had an idea, she was willing to reconnect. It didn't hurt that he was so lusciously attractive.

"Sure, you can get in touch," she agreed.

"What's your room number?"

Okay. Maybe he was hoping to hook up after all. Was he planning to show up at her room unannounced? Was that the price of cookies? She wasn't ready to give him that level of access. Whatever might happen between them, Olivia wanted to control the pace.

"My room number?" she questioned. "Just take my cell—I'm unlikely to spend much time sitting in my room. I've got a wedding to help prepare for."

"Oh. Right."

There was definite reluctance in his response. Why wouldn't they just exchange phone numbers? Presumably he wanted contact information. Something was odd.

He unzipped the black pouch slung across his body and pulled out two phones, then hesitated again, apparently struggling to choose between them. Was one a work phone? If so, why the struggle?

Weird.

"Okay, go ahead and type your info." He held out a phone.

"Why don't you just tell me your number and I'll text you, so you have mine?" she countered. Two could play at this game.

He took a deep breath as if the suggestion wasn't one he liked. Did he have a girlfriend? She decided to give him a chance to be honest.

"Don't want your girlfriend to catch you with someone else's number?"

The question appeared to take him by surprise.

"No. I don't have a girlfriend," he insisted. "That's not it."

As if to prove the point, he committedly rattled off a series of digits. She sent a text with her name. The message popped up—but not on the phone he'd first offered. What was the difference between his two phones? She couldn't let it go.

"So I made the cut?" she guessed.

"It's complicated." He sighed. "But yes. I don't typically…well… I mean… Please don't share my number with anyone, okay?"

"Okay…" she said, still baffled. "I'm not sure who would be asking me for your number, but I'll keep it to myself."

"Thank you."

She was so distracted by the question of why he would have such privacy concerns that she didn't once contemplate death on the motorcycle ride back to the hotel.

When they pulled up in the alley behind the hotel, Olivia dismounted the bike, suspecting her inner thighs might feel it the next day. They both removed their helmets, and Nikos resecured hers to the back of the bike.

He faced her, and the moment became awkward with the ambiguity of their outing. Nikos paid for lunch—did that make it a date? She still wasn't sure.

"Thanks again…"

"So I guess I'll…"

They both spoke at the same time, then laughed.

"Go ahead…" he insisted.

"I just want to thank you for everything today. It's been great…"

"Don't thank me yet. Wait until we get your cookies."

We? Was there going to be a *we*? Or was it just a language thing?

"Yeah, that would be awesome," she said. He sounded serious. Maybe it wasn't a false promise, maybe there was hope for cookies yet. Was there hope for anything more with him?

"Nikos, I will understand if you can't get any cookies."

"Trust me," he said. "I'll take care of them. I'll text you later with the details."

Okay, she thought. Obviously, he meant well, which was more than she would expect from a guy. Give him an A for effort. And appearance.

Nikos was still on the bike. Olivia would need

to step closer if their outing was indeed a date and a goodbye kiss was warranted. But if it wasn't a date? She'd be embarrassingly up in his face.

With split-second courage, she decided to kiss him.

She took a step closer, and his cologne teased her senses again.

"Like I said, um, thank you. I had a really good time today," she murmured, hoping he'd take a hint. "I appreciate your help."

He didn't pull away.

God, his eyes were intense. They widened and held her gaze. He clearly recognized what she intended, and a slow, encouraging grin spread across his face. Okay. He wanted it, too.

She licked her upper lip. Bit her lower lip. Delicious anticipatory tension flared between them, and she nearly giggled at the nervous delight of it. What was it about this guy that made her act like an idiot?

"Yeah, today was..." His voice trailed off with a deep inhalation. He lifted his hand and brushed her cheek with the back of his fingers. She slightly leaned into his caress. Damn. If she were a cat, she'd be purring.

Did he feel all fluttery, too? Or as a gorgeous guy on a sexy bike, was this just what he expected from a girl? Was it just what he did? Even if he wasn't great at pickup lines, surely he had frequent opportunities to kiss plenty of girls. Was this a typical encounter?

He cradled the nape of her neck and leaned infinitesimally closer, their foreheads nearly touching, his breath warm on her lips. He was showing incredible restraint, not greedily taking the kiss so clearly offered. Perhaps he didn't take it for granted at all. The pause was torturous. It was maddening. It was totally hot.

Olivia slid an encouraging hand along the smooth skin of his bicep. Although she'd innocently clutched his waist all day, this touch was an invitation. He accepted.

His mouth took hers, and she nearly groaned. He tasted heavenly; his lips were divine, moving in perfect harmony with hers, his tongue teasing deeper. In their sensuous exchange, there was no awkwardness or first-time weirdness. Instead, it was an indulgent, lazy, utterly perfect kiss. An open-mouthed, soul-stirring, time-stopping kiss. One with no demands but a tantalizing promise of future pleasures. Dear God, had there ever been such a first kiss? Not in her experience.

It should have scared her to death, experiencing such a profound kiss with someone she barely knew. But she wasn't scared. In fact, she realized it was the kind of kiss she could get very used to.

When they finally separated, Olivia opened her eyes, dazed and dazzled. A distinct look of satisfaction spread across Nikos's face, too. She wasn't sure if it was her imagination, but he appeared to be equally awestruck.

"I will see you again soon," he promised.

It was definitely a date.

MONDAY EVENING

After an abbreviated workout, Nikos, still full of adrenaline, ricocheted around his hotel suite. Reliving the unexpectedly vulnerable kiss was amazing…but agitating. He vacillated between euphoria at the intense suspicion that Olivia Keller was someone he would like to kiss forever and alarm at what those feelings implied. Since Athena, he had refused anything beyond a superficial relationship. Now he was losing his mind over the most perfect kiss he'd ever experienced… The possibilities whirled.

He needed energy-absorbent racetrack barriers. Not that he made a habit of crashing his car into the walls, but barriers were there, just in case. They kept a driver safe when he got too rash. And right now, Nikos felt as though he'd careened well past safety, through the gravel, and was headed toward a wall. He knew precisely how to straddle the line between recklessness and victory in a race car, but a true romantic relationship was a different story. He'd played it safe for so many years; now he felt a crazy, impulsive desire for a girl he'd only known for twenty-four hours! Who would leave in less than a week!

Was it wise to take such a risk?

He reminded himself that normal people do this every day. They meet someone who surprises and intrigues them. They flirt. They kiss. They exchange contact information. They text. Normal people did not have their staff arrange their romantic affairs. Normal people gambled and opened their hearts, sometimes trusting strangers on nothing more than an instinctual attraction.

Was he ready for that? At least the cookie situation gave him an excuse. But who would have thought securing baked goods would be so difficult? Did people deal with this kind of annoyance all the time? Apparently so. He felt foolish, realizing how far he'd disassociated from life beyond the track. If he genuinely wanted a real relationship that mirrored that of his parents, he needed to learn how to live in a world that didn't cater to his every whim. True, his parents had enough money to make things happen. But as a couple, they were grounded by family. His parents were humble, hardworking, and wholly committed to one another. Not that he wasn't hardworking, but he'd forged a solitary path for so long, eager to build an individual identity distinct from his family, that he'd almost convinced himself he was fine alone. But now, meeting Olivia Keller reminded him of what he was missing in his life.

For the first time in years, the power of a kiss

and the electrifying high-speed sensation of two bodies pressed against one another tempted Nikos to recklessly imagine a relationship with a woman who wasn't a celebrity orbiting him in a publicity-driven universe. A woman with whom he could share a home. A life. Far from fans. Away from the spotlight.

Was it possible? Could this fledgling relationship be something special? Something personal? Private.

And for that matter, how did he go about it? He needed a strategy.

During their first encounter, he'd imagined Olivia with ocean sunlight glinting off her hair. Now Nikos had an idea, even though he knew he should keep his expectations in check. Likely, once she discovered his true identity, their connection would sour no matter how unaffected he imagined her to be. But for the time being, he needed to be her Greek baker for at least another day. He wanted to live the fantastic dream of getting to know a woman who liked him simply for himself.

He texted Bryson.

I'll bake cookies on yacht if you clear tomorrow—don't argue just do it

Why? don't forget VIP event in an hour, so let's make cookies after that...

...and ok, I will cancel everything tomorrow

Nikos couldn't quite answer the initial question; he simply trusted Bryson to make it happen without explanation.

He debated his next move—call or text? Okay, maybe call. He needed to hear the tone of her voice. Texts were too ambiguous, too hard to read.

He found her number—not hard to do as there were so few others on his private phone.

Deep breath. He tapped the Call icon. His heart rate accelerated with each unanswered ring.

"Hello, this is Olivia..." He grinned at her American accent and breezy tone on the recording. *"Clearly, I don't want to talk to you right now... just kidding... But don't leave a message. I never check my inbox. Please call back later or text me..."*

How did people do this? Okay, text.

Hi this is Nikos

He was an idiot. He backspaced over his name and sent it. She knew who the text was from; he was already in her phone.

He waited, anticipatory energy building as if waiting for lights out to cue the start of a race.

Hi—sorry I didn't answer—meeting w/ wedding florist

Whew. Quick breath. Okay.

Can you txt me the cookies you need? recipes?

If I told you, I'd have to kill you. grandma recipes = top secret

Then no cookies for you

JK—I'll take pics and send—recipes are all hand-written. good luck with that

How many cookies do you need?

60 guests... 5 or 6 per guest...so 360 cookies? 30 doz?

!! that's a lot of cookies

Too many? I'll take less—whatever you can do

I can do 30 doz

The conversation paused.

Seriously?!!!! you are AWESOME

A torrent of happiness ran through his body. Now to the most crucial question.

Want to go on a boat w me tomorrow?

A long pause. Had he overplayed his hand? The uncertainty of waiting for her answer was exhilarating.

Speedboat? will I need a helmet?! pls say no

He laughed.

No speedboat no helmet just bathing suit…sea + sun = good vibes

That got a thumbs-up.

Omg, perfect, no bridesmaid duties tomorrow. I'd love to

Nikos grinned like an idiot. This was not his typical race-week preparation, and there would be hell to pay with Bryson, Aleko, the Segno Rosso team, and sponsors, but he couldn't have cared less. He'd never invited a woman to spend the whole day alone with him on his boat, but he suspected Olivia Keller was like no other woman he'd ever met.

Meet at same time/place as this morning, if that works

Sounds good. I like sea + sun vibes—see you tomorrow :-)

Nikos texted Aleko, hoping the old man would refrain from asking questions. He would disapprove of anything or anyone that distracted Nikos from racing.

Get day boat ready to take out tomorrow AM—include wine & food

Okay why? What are you doing?

Nikos had absolutely no idea what he was doing, but it was the most excitement he'd had off the track for as long as he could remember.

As the evening sun set over Port Hercules, Olivia graciously accepted another glass of champagne from one of countless black-clad servers circulating on the immense luxury superyacht owned by Stefano's firm. The only larger boat in the harbor was a behemoth that occupied the next slip. It was so big it blocked her view of the sea, which was annoying. *Wealthy men must suffer from yacht envy*, Olivia thought.

She snagged another *barbagiuan*, a ridiculously good cheese-and-spinach pastry that was evidently a Monegasque specialty.

She was brushing the crumbs from her cleavage when Maggs sidled up to her. "My dress looks good on you."

Olivia rolled her eyes. "If by *good* you mean *showcases my chest because it's too tight…*"

"At least you have boobs." Maggie shrugged. "And now, because I am your friend, I will introduce you to Stefano's friends. Unless you've made an undying vow to your Greek-motorcycle-baker boy and aren't interested."

Her sarcasm was obvious, as Maggie had never known Olivia to express a genuine commitment to any guy. But now, Olivia felt an uncharacteristic urge to defend Nikos rather than respond with the usual smart-aleck retort.

"Not undying vows yet…but Maggie, it's bizarre, because there is something there. Something different. We chatted all through lunch, and the way he listened to me… I felt like I'd known him forever. Like I could trust him."

"What?" Maggie demanded. "Who are you and what have you done with Olivia?!"

"I know," Olivia admitted. "Here's what's crazy…after Nikos shuttled me all over to look for cookies, I suddenly realized that my dad would never do anything like that for me. Nor would Sebastian. Or anyone else I've ever dated. Until Nikos, it hadn't occurred to me that a guy would be willing to do something nice without making me feel obligated. I mean, you would do anything for me. I would do anything for you. But that kind of gracious selflessness and generosity from a man? Never. Until today. It was an aha moment. It snuck up on me, and then I was like, *Oh, okay. This is how it should be. This is how a decent man should behave.* Who knew?"

"You aren't wrong. That is absolutely how a man should behave. Not that you would know, given your history with your dad. But Liv, don't swing too far the other way, gush over a guy, and get your heart broken just because someone is nice.

You don't know this guy Nikos. Be careful. Spending the whole day on a boat? I'm not saying don't do it..." She paused. "Liv, you've had some travel flings, but this sounds different. I love you, and I don't want to see you hurt."

"I appreciate your concern, Mags, but believe me," Olivia insisted, "after that kiss, I'm ready for whatever happens on the boat..."

Maggie raised her eyebrows knowingly.

"Yes, if *that* happens, it will be good. I'm sure of it. And seriously, Nikos is nothing like my father or Sebastian. He's different. I can feel it. I trust him. I mean, that kiss. A kiss like that doesn't lie."

That got another look.

"Even so"—Maggie rolled her eyes—"let me introduce you to Stefano's friends. Just in case."

They approached a group of handsome men in exquisitely tailored linen suits coupled with sockless suede loafers. They were hotly debating the upcoming race.

"I'm telling you, Leonikaros is done..."

"No, he desperately wants this last win in Monaco..."

"He may want it, but Mancinelli is hot on his tail—and both teams are tied for points...and Leonikaros's seat will be up for grabs next year."

"Gentlemen," Maggie interrupted. "As much as I'd love to discuss F1 drama with you, I want to introduce you to my best friend, Olivia Keller..."

Twenty minutes later, Olivia had concluded that European bros were just as annoying as American bros, albeit these ones had more money and were thus more obnoxious than the guys she usually met over drinks. Admittedly, she had herself to blame as she typically gravitated toward guys who shared her aversion to forever commitments, wedding bells, and white picket fences.

The contrast to Nikos was striking. She marveled at the miracle of meeting the only guy in Monaco who wasn't so wealthy that he couldn't get past his own self-importance.

She quickly extricated herself from the racing-obsessed bro-fest and engaged in a far more interesting conversation with Stefano's aunt and uncle. As Uncle Klaus was a long-time racing aficionado, the couple planned to stay in Monaco after the wedding for the Grand Prix. Aunt Kiki asked Olivia questions about her life in New York City before the charming older couple excused themselves to return to the hotel.

As the other guests also said good-night, Olivia contentedly stood near the deck railing, waiting for Maggie and Stefano to make the rounds. The tranquil ocean under the moonlight was magical. How amazing it would be to spend the night on the sea, under the infinite sky. The planned daytime outing with Nikos was exciting—she was uncharacteristically giddy imagining it. And that kiss? What might it lead to? This wedding trip was proving to be far more exciting than expected. She had no complaints.

As Olivia waited, she watched with mild curiosity as a few men appeared on the deck of the neighboring superyacht. It took a moment, but then she looked more closely, and her interest piqued. One guy moved in a smooth, familiar way. He had a recognizable silhouette.

But what was he doing on the gigantic boat? She whipped out her phone and texted.

Look to your left

The phone in Nikos's back pocket buzzed. His private phone. He knew it was her before he looked and felt a surge of inexplicable happiness.

But then he read the text, and his heart thudded against his ribcage. Slowly, he turned.

Across the dark water gap, she stood on the deck of a nearby yacht, her hair dancing in the breeze and her body beautifully illuminated by moonlight. The gorgeous image sucked the air right out of his lungs. Why did she have this effect on him?

As much as he wanted to simply enjoy the sight, he found himself mentally scrambling once again for an explanation. He took a few of the calming breaths he so often practiced with his trainer.

Okay. If he could maintain his wits at two hundred miles per hour, he could bluff through this.

She'd clearly recognized him, so he couldn't just disappear. He gamely waved. She returned the gesture. Now, how to explain his presence on the most expensive boat in the harbor? She'd mentioned she was headed to a cocktail party that evening, but it never occurred to him that it would be on the neighboring yacht.

Hi gorgeous

Lame, but that would at least buy a moment to think up a story…any story…an excuse.

What's with the big boat? moving up in the world?

Part-time 2nd job, don't tell my boss

Damn I thought NYC was expensive but Monaco must be crazy—side gigs suck

Relieved that she seemed to accept—and even sympathize—with his explanation, further inspiration took him.

Hold on

He pulled out his phone, saved a cut-down version of the cookie-baking content Bryson had just produced, and sent it to her.

Making your cookies in boat's galley—decided to add another variety…

…Greek cookies are the best

He waited. He could tell from her silhouette that she was watching the video. He trusted she wouldn't realize the Segno Rosso shirt he wore in the video was an exclusive driver jersey.

Then she looked up.

Even across the water, he knew she was smiling. It was as if she were only millimeters away, and he could feel the pleasure and warmth in her gaze. It undid him.

Love the video you are too cute

Until she'd exploded into his life, he'd had no idea he wanted someone to look at him with such fondness. He was used to awe. To adulation and greed, as though he were a gilded prize rather than a living, breathing person with feelings. But her gaze was completely different, unlike anything he'd felt in a long time, if ever. Now, for a crazy second, it was as if he would prefer her affectionate expression over standing on a podium before thousands of cheering spectators and millions of rapt TV viewers. Those people didn't celebrate him with their idolization. They merely affirmed the curated image he represented. The fans saw the F1 driver. Olivia saw Nikos. And, incredibly, she liked what she saw. Could this connection become something more?

He suspected he would know when they spent time alone on the sea. No phones, no interruptions. Just the two of them. It was a miracle that she had agreed to go on the boat. She didn't know him; he never let anyone get so close on such short acquaintance. But something about her made him willing to drop his usual caution.

All cookies will be ready on thursday AM

Incredible! You seriously are the best!! see you tomorrow—can't wait! :)

Maybe it was the night air or the full moon, but he couldn't help himself.

I really liked kissing you

Even as he sent it, he panicked. Too honest?

Me, too. Maybe we should do it again?

Oh hell yes.

That can be arranged…

…are you headed back to the hotel? Want an escort?

…protection from the mean streets of Monte Carlo

He heard her laughter echo across the water.

Another stellar pickup attempt…

...I'm going to wait for my friends and walk back with them

...but maybe more kisses tomorrow ;-)

I'm gonna hold you to that

Even as he thrilled at the exchange, an irritating little voice in his head reminded him that sooner or later, he would have to tell her the truth. And when he did, would she still see him the same way, still want to kiss him? Or would it all explode in his face?

TUESDAY MORNING

FOR THE SECOND MORNING, Nikos waited for Olivia outside the service entrance, eager to be on their way. He hoped she'd be prompt; he didn't like sitting exposed outside the hotel. Fortunately, right on time, the back door opened and she appeared, radiant in the early light. As she sashayed down the alley, smiling that glorious smile, she suddenly paused and pulled out her buzzing phone.

"Oh! Oh my gosh! My suitcase has finally arrived!" She looked up. "It was delayed because of the strike. Do you mind if I go back up to my hotel room for a second? I can get my sunblock and a few other things…"

Nikos wavered. He could ride around while waiting for her. Would she think that was strange? Impatient? Rude?

"You can come up, if you want," she offered. "I'll only be a minute or two."

Nikos dismounted and parked the bike near the door. Out of habit, he put on his sunglasses and pulled his hood up.

"Keep an eye on the bike," he murmured to the security guard, who nodded in agreement.

He followed Olivia down the service corridor. As expected, she headed directly for the public elevator, chatting about the outfits she'd had to make do without. He wondered why she hadn't simply purchased replacement clothing. And he wondered if she was so talkative because she was as excited as he was for their planned outing.

The elevator doors closed, and Olivia hit the appropriate floor button. Nikos stood behind her, head down, praying no one else would get on.

No such luck. As Olivia mentioned something about peanut butter, which he understood to be an American delicacy, the elevator stopped in the hotel lobby. Two men and a young boy got on. Olivia greeted them with a polite "Good morning." Nikos hoped the distraction of a beautiful woman would hold their attention. Eyes glued to the floor, he held his breath. *Keep looking forward*, he willed them. *Keep looking forward.*

When the elevator arrived at her floor, Olivia exited, and Nikos made to follow. As he hastily trailed her down the hall, he heard the child's excited voice in French: *"Papa! Vois-tu qui c'est..."*

Did Olivia know enough French to realize the little boy had recognized him? Thankfully, the elevator doors closed before his cover was blown.

They entered Olivia's hotel room. Nikos hung back, not wanting to invade her privacy. Even so, he was mesmerized by the intimacy of the turned-back bed covers, the cosmetic jumble spilled across the credenza, and the towel tossed over the chair back. In the small room, her presence hung in the air like perfume. He suspected the spaces he occupied weren't as revealing of his personality, merely his identity.

"Oh, thank God," she exclaimed as she hoisted the suitcase onto the bench at the foot of the bed and unzipped it. It was filled with tidy pouches. Nikos watched, curious, as she rifled through the bag. He never packed his own gear. The crew was responsible for the enormously complicated task of packing the car, the tools, the electronics, the building structures, and all of the garage components. Bryson arranged for someone to handle Nikos's clothing and the few belongings he required when traveling from race to race. The most Nikos ever personally carried was a backpack with the bare minimum of what he needed to tune out the accompanying circus.

"You are going to need this." Olivia turned and held out a plastic tub.

"And this is…?"

"The peanut butter!" she exclaimed. "Maggie asked me to bring it. I didn't know it was for cookies. You'll need it for the Peanut Butter Blossoms—the cookies that have chocolate drops in the middle. You should use Hershey Kisses, but you may have to make do with Swiss chocolate."

"A hardship, to be sure." He laughed. She smirked at him.

“Is peanut butter used only for cookies?” he asked.

“No.” She shook her head. “It’s like Nutella. You put it on toast or bagels. It’s amazing on ice cream. I’m not going to lie—I’ve been known to eat peanut butter straight from the jar.”

He envisioned her life, her days and nights in her apartment in New York City. He quirked an eyebrow. “I need to taste this peanut butter.”

“Oh, you do, do you?” she replied. Her voice dropped to a sultry hint.

He wasn’t exactly sure what she was proposing…but he would gladly agree to whatever it was.

She dipped her chin and opened the jar. She swiped her finger and extended it to him without breaking eye contact.

His mouth went dry. Was she really inviting him to…

He leaned forward, eyes still locked. He closed his lips and curled his tongue around her proffered finger. As he sucked on it, she slowly, suggestively drew it out of his mouth. She lightly touched his lip, traces of unreadable emotions playing across her face. He forgot how to breathe. The world stopped.

Until the taste hit him. It was awful.

Furthermore, he couldn’t say anything profound because his tongue was stuck to the roof of his mouth. He frowned and tried to swallow the stuff while she dissolved into laughter, breaking the moment’s intensity.

"Oh my God, you should see your face," she hooted. "I'm sorry—I had to do it."

"That is clearly an acquired taste," he admitted, making inelegant but necessary movements to reclaim use of his mouth and jaw.

"Don't be insulted, but the funniest thing in the world is feeding a dog peanut butter and watching them try to slurp it down," she admitted. "I had to see how a person who had never tried it would react."

"I'm not going to ask who is more amusing, me or the dog," he said.

She laughed harder. Humor was so cultural. Was she teasing him for fun? Was this a good sign? He'd down a whole jar of the vile goo if it endeared him to her.

"I love dogs," she said with a smile. "They are loyal and authentic in their enthusiasm. They live in the moment. If people were more like dogs, we'd all be much happier."

"I love dogs, too. We always had them when I was growing up." He then fixed her with a stern look. "But you took advantage of my innocence by feeding me that nasty stuff. You'll be sorry when my family serves you lamb's head for Easter. And as a special guest, I will make sure you are honored with the eyeballs."

She grimaced, laughing, then caught his gaze.

They both froze, wary of the moment's intimacy and all that the prospect of spending a holiday together implied.

* * *

Later that morning, after a motorcycle ride at a nerve-wracking speed along the spectacular coast, they arrived at the charming French town of Beaulieu-sur-Mer. Olivia would have loved to explore, but Nikos was focused on their excursion. She followed him briskly down the long wooden dock in Porte de Fourmis. It was a tiny harbor compared to the superyacht parking lot in Monte Carlo and felt more down-to-earth. As they approached the boat, several people called out enthusiastic greetings in rapid French. Everyone seemed to know Nikos.

"I've been in New York too long," Olivia admitted. "People in Pittsburgh are more like the people here. Everyone talks to everyone else, including strangers. It's nice."

"Very friendly," Nikos agreed, although Olivia noticed he didn't respond to everyone's greetings. Perhaps he was generally reserved, although he hadn't been shy with her. And now she had an entire day to get to know him better. How much better remained to be seen.

The boat was gorgeous—a gleaming forty-foot Cranchi cabin cruiser. Nikos explained the small yacht was perfect for a day trip or a weekend on the water. Olivia took his word for it. The only boating she'd ever done was on a pontoon on her hometown's three rivers or taking the Staten Island Ferry.

At Nikos's invitation, Olivia lounged on a rear bench and watched him bustle about, casting off the lines connecting them to the dock. Sure-footed, he moved back and forth effortlessly, confidently from dock to boat. The sun gleamed in his hair and bounced brilliantly off his sunglasses.

"How do you know how to do all this?" she wondered.

"I'm Greek," he explained. "I've got saltwater in my veins."

"Whose boat is this?"

"Umm..." He hesitated. "The same person who owns the superyacht."

Olivia figured it was up to Nikos to determine whether taking out the boat was permitted. She was happy to go along for the ride as long as she didn't miss the wedding because she was in a French jail for stealing a yacht. Her budget wouldn't cover bail.

Nikos took up the helm as the engines below shuddered to life. They backed away from the dock, and he detached the final line. With a broad smile at Olivia, he steered toward the open sea, utterly in command and clearly in his natural element. Olivia was delightfully out of her element but loving every minute. One could get used to this life, she mused. One could get used to spending time with this man.

Keeping his eyes on the horizon, Nikos nudged off his burgundy Adidas. Olivia had always felt there was something particularly intimate and vulnerable about a guy in bare feet. Seeing Nikos without his shoes confirmed it.

His T-shirt was the next piece of clothing to be shed.

Olivia gawked. Holy Lord.

His skin was tinted with an olive-bronze undertone, a blessing of his Mediterranean heritage. A tangle of gold chain, leather cording, and beads draped around his neck. A tapestry of tattoos accentuated and glorified the sculpted musculature on his back. Did he realize how alluring he was?

"That's some serious artwork you've got," she commented.

He stiffened almost infinitesimally, and she wondered if she'd embarrassed him. But then he shot a curious glance over his shoulder.

"Do you like it?"

"I do," she said. She'd never dated a guy with such extensive tattoos. Then again, she'd also not gone sailing off the coast of France. She could adapt to both. Easily. Happily.

"Will you tell me about them?"

"Greek cross on this arm. Greek key design here," he explained, pointing at each bicep in turn. "The big tattoo on my upper back shows the Resurrection based on an ancient Greek mosaic called the Anastasis. My mother disapproved of me getting tattoos but couldn't say no because of the subject matter."

"I see." She laughed, itching to trace the intricate design with her finger. "I've been to Greek churches for food festivals and seen icons in that style. Very cool. What are the squiggly tattoos along your waist?" It was another area of his body that invited her touch.

He paused before he answered. "Racing circuit maps."

"Racing circuits like the upcoming one in Monte Carlo?"

He nodded and made a noncommittal noise. "Mm-hmm."

"Why the dates?"

Another pause. "I was at those races on those dates."

Okay. The man was a major fan but hesitant to admit it. Olivia didn't care one way or another and was impressed he didn't blab on and on like most guys would about their sports obsessions.

"You must really be into racing. Where is each particular tattoo from?"

Reaching behind his back, he touched each image with his thumb and rattled off cities on every continent except Antarctica. Monte Carlo was above his right hip.

While ambivalent about racing, Olivia was impressed at the extent of his globe-hopping. She loved to travel, and Nikos had evidently seen the world. She wasn't sure how a baker could afford such travel, but then again, he worked two jobs. Maybe he traveled inexpensively as part of the superyacht's crew.

"None from the United States?"

"Nope. But there are a few races there. I hope to add one or two of them soon."

"I see. So, do you generally enjoy traveling, or is it all about the races?"

"Both." He stretched, rolling his shoulders and twisting his neck. Olivia was fascinated by the way the movement rippled through the images on his back. From the captain's seat, he turned toward her, lightly keeping one hand on the helm. The motion accentuated his abs, which were every bit as mouthwatering as his back.

Not wanting to be caught blatantly staring, she turned toward the water and smoothed back the hair that blew free from her braid. Without a word, Nikos opened a storage compartment and produced a cap with a Segno Rosso racing logo. He handed it to her.

Somehow, that simple, thoughtful gesture appealed to her even more than the tantalizing glimpse of his body or their sweet kiss the day before. It would be all too easy to fall for a man who anticipated and responded to her needs before she even asked. One who was willing to run her all over the city to find baked goods for a wedding he wasn't attending, for a couple he had never met. As she'd explained to Maggie, his graciousness and attentiveness were unprecedented...and incredibly sexy.

"What do you think of Monte Carlo?" he asked, drawing her attention back to their travel conversation.

Olivia paused, then decided to be honest. "Monaco is an odd place," she said. "It's beautiful, but it's so unreal. That cocktail party I was at last night? It was insane. Superyachts, private helicopters, couture, sports cars? I mean, who lives like that? In real life?"

An odd look passed over Nikos's face.

"Maybe you don't notice how bizarre it is. You must see that kind of opulence all the time, at the hotel and on the yacht where you work. How do you deal with the crazy wealth? If you grew up on a small Greek island, it's got to be strange, right?" she persisted.

He turned to the horizon, reflecting. "Money doesn't make a difference to me. I think life is what you experience. And there are many different ways to live in the world."

Olivia considered this. "True. And in New York, I see it all. Wealthy people, poor people. Mostly, people like you and me, just scrambling to get by. Even though I don't travel as much as I would like, I am surrounded by people from every corner of the globe, which is cool. I think you're right. There are many different ways to live in the world."

He nodded, seemingly lost in thought.

After a comfortable, companionable silence, Nikos steered them into a cove of translucent, calm, turquoise water. He cut the engine on the boat and gestured to the ocean.

"Do you want to swim?"

"Absolutely!" Olivia agreed.

He dropped anchor and then pulled two foam rafts from a storage compartment. He tossed them into the water and lowered a ladder from the back platform.

Olivia pulled off her cover-up. Although he wasn't blatant about it, she knew Nikos appreciated the sight of her in a bathing suit. And she, in turn, enjoyed his appreciation. She also knew some women in the Mediterranean went topless at the beach. She would if they were on a crowded beach with a thousand other people. But alone, with just Nikos? Going topless would escalate whatever might happen between them. Perhaps she was only postponing the inevitable, but she wasn't quite ready to take the next step. Although she did have every intention of repeating that kiss.

"Best way to get in the water? Should I go down the ladder or…?" she asked.

Nikos flashed a wicked grin, took two steps, and effortlessly executed a perfect flip over the side of the boat. She peered into the water to watch him surface, sleek as a seal, and sluice water over his head to slick back his hair. His performance made her flush with appreciation…and a few other heated emotions. Damn, he was gorgeous.

"Okay, well, that's not going to happen."

She moved to the edge of the platform, squeezed her arms over her chest, covered her face, pinched her nose, and jumped. She came up from the water, sputtering. "Not as graceful as you, but wow, this water feels good."

They circled each other, grinning like idiots, treading water, lolling in the gentle ebb and flow.

"Do you want a raft?" Nikos pushed one toward her. He hoisted himself easily onto his; Olivia floundered. Nikos laughed. It was at her expense, but it was a delightful sound.

"This is payback for the peanut butter, isn't it?" she panted, finally coming to rest on her stomach after a few failed attempts. "Unlike you, I'm not part dolphin. I grew up inland."

Their rafts bobbed in the undulating current. Nikos, his eyes shut, held loosely to a line tied to the boat, his other hand dangling in the crystalline water.

"Give me your hand," he murmured lazily, extending his. "So if we fall asleep, you don't drift away."

Keeping one arm as a pillow, she stretched out and hooked her fingers around his. As they touched, he opened his eyes, their hue mirroring the azure sea. His expression was fathomless. Then, without letting go of her hand, he shut his eyes and tipped his face back toward the sun.

"So tell me more about your job..." he prompted.

Olivia moaned. "I'm drifting in a Mediterranean paradise, and you ask about my job. That's kind of a buzzkill, you know?"

"Sorry." He grinned. "I'm curious. Did you go to school to learn how to do it?"

Olivia laughed. "Nope. I fell into it. I studied philosophy. Love the ancient Greeks."

He opened his eyes and quirked a curious eyebrow. "I think you must be a very smart person, Olivia Keller."

"What about you?"

"Me?"

"Do you see anyone else out here on a raft? Yes, Nikos, you. Did you go to culinary school?"

He took a deep breath and exhaled. She waited for his story while admiring how the light illuminated his profile and seductive lips. Oh, she wanted to taste those lips again.

"I didn't go to culinary school. I've known what I've wanted to do since I was a kid. You could say I learned by doing. I trained all over Europe."

"I could tell you love baking when you made me that video. There was a lot of joy in it. It must be nice to know exactly what you want to be. Unlike me. No kid says they want to go into insurance when they grow up."

"I suppose not," he said. "But now I find myself facing a serious question, and I don't have your philosophical background to help me decide what to do next."

"What do you mean?" she asked.

"My contract is up in December. It's time to make a major career change and do something different with my life. I've always been goal-driven, but I don't know what to do next. My father would love me to be part of the family shipping business along with my sisters. I'm not sure that's what I want, though."

"Goals aren't everything. I've always been a fly-by-the-seat-of-my-pants kind of girl, but I've made it work," Olivia offered.

"'Fly by the seat of my pants'..." he repeated slowly. "I'm not so familiar with that phrase. Not sure I follow what you mean."

"It means you don't have a plan or a long-term goal. You rely on instinct. You just make the best decision possible at each critical junction and keep moving forward."

"I see." He raised an eyebrow. "I hoped it meant someone who would enjoy going fast on a motorcycle."

"Nice try." She laughed.

"Hmm," he pondered. "So, is that your particular approach, or is it an American thing?"

Olivia sighed. How much should she explain?

"I'd say it's my circumstance. I grew up with a lot of uncertainty. My dad was selfish and unpredictable—a total narcissist and only around when he wanted to play at being the perfect family. We couldn't rely on him. He lied about everything. Made promises and broke them. Did whatever suited him, with no consideration for how it might impact us. For example, he signed a lease with my mom, then defaulted. She and I had to move, and I bounced around to different schools. He'd reappear, apologetic and charming, and she'd take him back. The cycle would repeat.

"Don't get me wrong—my mom is an amazing woman. She did her best to protect me, and I appreciate all her sacrifices. But our life wasn't one in which we could plan ahead. We couldn't rely on my dad. We had to figure it out as we went along. Not surprisingly, I didn't know what I wanted to be when I grew up. I just knew I never wanted to be dependent on anyone else. I wanted to be able to take care of myself, but I wasn't sure how. Then in high school, I wrote an essay on Socrates and got a full scholarship. Great! I didn't have to depend on my dad for tuition. But when I graduated, I discovered nobody hires philosophy majors to sit around and ponder, so I had to talk my way into a job I wasn't technically qualified for. But that's what New York City is all about, right? Making something from nothing, reinventing yourself."

He opened one eye. "Maybe that's what I need to do—reinvent myself in New York City."

Her heart hiccupped. "Then you'll have to look me up when you're in town."

Nikos was dropping hints all over the place that whatever they were doing, he didn't view it as a quick fling. Olivia didn't think his words were sheer flattery—he appeared sincere. But should she encourage him? Could she believe him? And why did it matter? Could she honestly imagine a relationship with someone who lived half a world away? Incredibly, every instinct said yes, for the first time in her life, this was someone she might trust. Someone who wouldn't flatter her with convenient lies, someone she could rely on.

"I am still really jet-lagged," Olivia murmured, shifting the conversation before it stretched into scary territory. "The travel is catching up with me. Tell me something else, so I don't fall asleep. Tell me a story…"

She waited to see how he would respond to that request. If he told her a story about racing or any other sport, she'd tip him right off his raft.

"A story…" His voice turned thoughtful. "I know some Greek myths. How about Eros and Psyche?"

That was a surprising and delightful offer.

"Perfect. I forget how that one goes."

Olivia basked in the warmth of the sun and the warmth of his voice as he told her the tale of the beautiful god sneaking incognito to pay conjugal visits to his doubting mortal wife and the punishment she endured for exposing him.

"I don't know if I like that story. I think she got a bad rap," Olivia argued when he reached the end of the tale. It reminded her of how her father punished her mom for his own failings. "Eros's expectations were unfair. I have no patience for people who need to test love to prove it exists. And what was she supposed to do when her lover wasn't truthful about who he was? Just forgive and trust him? Not a chance."

Nikos squeezed her hand. "At least the story has a happy ending. Try to keep that in mind." Olivia snorted but didn't argue.

After another extended silence, dozing and floating in the warm sunlight, Olivia sighed. "I think my back is burning. I should probably get into some shade."

They rolled off their rafts, Nikos with far more grace. As Olivia struggled to hoist herself out of the water and up the ladder onto the swaying boat, Nikos placed a hand on her rear and gave her a boost.

Once safely on the deck, she turned to where he floated below.

"Was that you being helpful or a poorly disguised excuse to grab my ass?" She raised a flirtatious eyebrow.

"Absolutely."

He smiled broadly from the water, and her heart turned upside down.

Sailing once again, Olivia relaxed, and Nikos steered the boat to another spectacular and seemingly unpopulated section of the coast.

"This is a good place to stop for a while. If you are hungry, I brought food."

"Fantastic. I'm starved," Olivia agreed. "Hey, but first, do you think you could get my back?"

She held out the sunblock. She wanted to ask before he was busy with the food…and before she lost her nerve. She'd spent the previous day wrapped around him. Sunblock assistance shouldn't be a big deal. But…

He took the tube, and she turned to face the ocean. Anticipating his touch, her stomach started crazy flip-flopping again. *It's just sunblock*, she silently repeated.

However, as soon as his palms settled warmly on her shoulders, she knew she was lying to herself.

Good heavens, the man had good hands. His touch was mesmerizing. He squeezed her shoulders like a deep-tissue massage. He worked the lotion into her skin, rubbing slow, sensuous circles over her entire back, inch by inch. He rested his hands on her hips, his thumbs tenderly working above the edge of her bikini bottom. Throughout, his warm breath caressed her neck.

His touch aroused every part of her body, and her entire being yearned for the same pleasured treatment he was bestowing on her back. She knew her quickened breathing revealed her feelings. It would be impossible for him not to realize the effect he was having. But what would he do about it? What should she do?

Just when she thought he would step away, he nestled his face in the spot where her neck met her shoulder. She held her breath. He nuzzled her skin and squeezed her hips. That did it; she was all in.

Encouragingly, Olivia twined her arms up and back around his neck. He brought his lips to her shoulder.

"About that kiss…" he murmured.

She twisted back, turning toward him, and discovered his mouth searching for hers. There was no hesitancy when they connected, just a devouring kiss of incredible longing, intensity, and passion. How could a kiss contain such richness? Such depth? It confirmed what she'd suspected after their first kiss—she'd never experienced this kind of physical passion with anyone. A kiss wasn't enough.

As their mouths moved in perfect cadence, she leaned back into Nikos and felt the irrefutable evidence of how badly he wanted her. Ridiculously pleased, she smiled against his lips. Growing bolder, his hands roved over her body, exploring the landscape of her figure. Enflamed by the increasing intimacy of his touch, she moaned softly. He moved to untie the back of her bikini top; she loosened the tie at her neck. The garment fell to the ground. Their encounter was escalating, and she had no intention of slowing down.

Now his hands could cradle her freely. She needed more. She needed all of him.

Too tormented to hold on to their kiss, she shut her eyes and relaxed her head back onto his chest, her arms still wrapped behind his head. The world was spinning. It was as if she were deliriously drunk on the intoxicating scent of salty air, sunblock, and the lingering hint of cologne.

He kept one hand on her breast, the other hand slid down her side, in answer to her silent plea. He lightly teased the top edge of her bikini bottom, and she involuntarily lifted her hips, urging him on.

With a decisive motion, his hand dropped lower. Even through the barrier of her bathing suit, the contact was electrifying. One direct caress and she would shatter. Desperately, she arched her back, silently begging. Finally, finally, he slipped his hand under the fabric. She clutched his neck as he simultaneously touched her and nipped at her shoulder with his teeth.

It was all she needed to peak. With his free arm, he held her tight, safe against his chest, until she caught her breath and came back to rational consciousness. Flush against his body, she felt a disconcerting bond she had never experienced with any other guy.

Was this what it felt like to fall in love?

The thought sent her spiraling into a blind panic.

What was happening?

It was too much. The experience…the feelings were too big. Yes, she'd fooled around with guys before. No harm, no foul. It happened. Sometimes it was fun. Sometimes it was awkward. Sometimes it led to something more. She had suspected her feelings for Nikos were adding up to something different. Something unprecedented. But never—never—had she been touched in a way that rocked her very soul.

Her body stilled, and Nikos sensed it. He carefully placed both hands on her hips. Olivia swallowed and drew her arms over her chest. She was too exposed. How in the hell was she going to get her bikini top back on…

"Here," he murmured.

He reached for his discarded T-shirt but stayed behind her as she accepted it, allowing her some privacy. Relieved, confused…she pulled the shirt over her head.

"Hey." He brushed her upper arm lightly as he

turned to face her. "I'm sorry. We shouldn't have… I shouldn't have…"

He looked a little dazed as well.

"No, no…" She squeezed her eyes shut, frustrated. What was wrong with her? Their interaction should not have been upsetting. At all. They'd both wanted it. After the delightful two days they'd spent together, it wasn't a surprise. She'd predicted it to Maggie. She'd eagerly imagined his hands all over her. Furthermore, their physical connection was incredible. She should be begging for more, not doing…whatever awkward thing she was doing.

She grabbed a beach towel and tossed it around her shoulders. She sank into the corner of the bench and crossed her legs tightly. Foot jangling nervously, she stared out over the water, embarrassed to look at him, trying to pull herself together.

She wasn't a prude. She'd had boyfriends. Situations. She'd had some flings and illicit encounters with pretty faces and successful flirts. She'd enjoyed travel romances and one-night stands. Her panic wasn't about the physical act. She'd had plenty of hot encounters with hot guys.

But the feelings Nikos provoked were beyond anything she'd known before. Even more disconcerting, she suspected those emotions might be reciprocated. He, too, might be feeling something profound. Was she ready to consider that? Had her life turned upside down before she'd realized it? With someone she'd leave behind in a few short days?

Intimacy with Nikos had unexpectedly opened a whole new realm, like they'd ignited something deeper, a truth that had always been theirs, simply waiting to be discovered. They'd clicked together like two missing puzzle pieces. It was perfect but overwhelming. She was both tempted and terrified. None of her exes ever made her feel this way. She'd intentionally chosen guys who wanted to keep their distance as much as she did. Now she was sailing into uncharted waters. And she didn't mean the Mediterranean.

She chanced a glimpse at Nikos. Not surprisingly, he looked confused.

"Nikos. Just give me a minute," she pleaded. "It's me—I am being stupid. I don't know why I'm reacting so… I don't know. Like this."

She heard him take a deep breath.

"Should I make us something to eat?" he offered. "My grandmother says that no matter what upsets you, you will always feel better if you eat something."

Olivia choked on a burst of nervous laughter. "My grandmother says the same thing. It's universal grandma wisdom. Food would be wonderful. Please. I'd like something to eat. That's probably it—I'm hungry and tired. I got a little overwrought. I'm sorry."

"Don't apologize," he said, squeezing her shoulder lightly, then descended the few steps to the lower deck.

As he disappeared, the tension drained from her

body. Okay. A Mediterranean fling was one thing. That she could easily enjoy.

But feeling as though she had met her soulmate? That hadn't been on the bingo card for this trip, this month, this year…this lifetime. Soulmates didn't exist. Love was a fantasy and a trap that nearly destroyed her mother. And love at first sight—or first touch?—absolutely didn't exist. That was a fairytale, and she'd never been a sucker for make-believe…until she met Nikos. How had this happened? And what should she do about it?

She heard him coming back up the steps. She took a deep breath. Which way did she want this to go?

He hovered, carrying a tray of something that looked and smelled delicious. Clearly, his Greek grandma knew her business.

Olivia tried to smile. "Thanks for the T-shirt. More racing gear, huh?"

"I have too much of it," he admitted. He unfolded a clever little table from a cabinet under the bench and set the tray on it.

"Salade Niçoise," he said. "Fresh bread. And wine. Berry galette for dessert."

"God, that looks divine." Olivia nodded as he offered wine and poured.

She took a bite. "Oh wow. You are an artist."

"Glad you like it. After we eat, we can head back to the harbor."

Olivia paused mid-bite and put down her fork. She looked out over the horizon, the sun well past its midpoint. It was a glorious view, a glorious day, with a glorious man.

Her day with Nikos was literally the stuff epic romances were made of. Was she brave enough to consider a romance? Not just a fling?

She'd overreacted. Now, was it too late to salvage the situation? Or should she shrug and acknowledge the chance had passed?

She realized she desperately didn't want their first attempt at intimacy to be their last.

They could hook up. If it was fantastic—and she had no doubt it would be—she would head home with some scintillating Monte Carlo memories. Or…if she really was in mortal danger of falling for this guy…well. She had never permitted herself that kind of surrender, but she wasn't a coward. She needed to understand what was happening, and there was only one way to find out.

"When you take out the boat, how long do you usually stay out?"

"That depends." He shrugged. "However long I want."

"You said you sometimes stay overnight?"

He stilled. "Yes, but I wasn't presuming we would…"

"I know. Do you have to be back tonight?"

"No…" he said slowly.

She knew she was bewildering him, even though it wasn't her intent to mess around or play games. She decided to be honest. She owed him that much.

"Nikos. The reason I pulled back isn't because I

didn't want to be with you. I pulled back because I do want you. Badly. And that scared me. Terrified me. I don't really know you. But I think I'm starting to really like you."

His eyes widened. She suspected she had shocked him with her honesty. He looked at her intently. "So, what are you saying?"

"I want to stay out all night. Here. On the boat. With you."

He caught his breath sharply, as if carefully weighing her words and proposition. Finally, he nodded and flashed that devastatingly sexy smile. "Okay. No matter what happens, I really like being with you, too. I want you to know that."

He reached across the table, pausing before he touched her face, giving her plenty of time to pull back. When she didn't, he caressed her cheek with a butterfly touch.

"Olivia Keller, how did you come crashing into my life? And what am I going to do with you?" He gently brushed the hair back from her temple. "But I'm glad we're here. We can do whatever you like."

TUESDAY EVENING

NIKOS FELT LIKE he'd flipped into a rollover. He'd only rolled a car twice in all his years as a driver. But when he had, it was a completely disorienting and terrifying experience. And like those hair-raising situations, he now suspected he might not emerge intact. Especially after encountering Olivia's whiplash emotions, he knew the safest move would be to chart a course back to Monte Carlo immediately.

But he'd never been one to stick to a conservative strategy behind the wheel. Why start now? Olivia said she wanted to stay out all night with him. Great. But what exactly did this girl want? Did she even know? What did he want? His desire for her was different from whatever he felt—or didn't feel—for the women he typically dated. But how deep was his desire? Did it extend to something more profound?

On top of his uncertainty, he also heard Bryson's nagging voice inside his head insisting that if they stayed out, Nikos would never get back in time for Media Day and all the other escalating pre-race commitments. It was a valid concern, but Nikos had no answer. Right now, his priority was seeing how the evening would unfold. He couldn't deny that he hoped it would include making love to Olivia Keller.

After they finished their meal, he opened another bottle of wine, grateful that there was more than one. Nikos never drank during the season, and after a day in the sun, on the water, and in the company of this unpredictable woman, he suspected the wine affected him more than usual, made him a bit more emotional. Perhaps more honest. Which was fine. The team nutritionist might kill him, and this was not how he should prepare for a race, but in the moment, he didn't regret a thing.

He refilled their glasses and studied Olivia over the rim of his wineglass as she untangled her hair with her fingers and loosely re-braided it. The unconscious gesture, arms lifted and stretching to reach the back of her head, mimicked the way she'd anchored her arms around his neck earlier, accelerating his body's instinctual need faster than his conscious mind could comprehend.

He was a driver. On the track, he made split-second decisions and took decisive action. But he also knew that his best split-second decisions were grounded in calculated, intentional planning.

But how could he have planned for this? His recent futile attempts at romance had been planned and pursued based mainly on a woman's image and appearance. All had been sadly dissatisfying.

Olivia appeared to have little interest in glamour.

Not that he was unaffected by her appearance. Far from it. The golden glow of a Mediterranean sunset illuminated her face and made her eyes shine. Tiny sun-dappled freckles danced across her nose. The outline of her breasts pushing against the thin fabric of his shirt was even more erotic than seeing her in a bikini top. She'd pulled her linen pants back on but wore them low on her hips. The still-visible strings of her bikini bottoms teased him to distraction, just begging to be untied. She wore no makeup, no jewelry, and despite her efforts to keep it contained, her hair waved riotously in the ocean breeze. She took his breath away.

Unlike the other women he'd dated, her appearance didn't seem to be the cornerstone of her identity. He liked that. Her essence enthralled him. She was resilient, confident, and intelligent. A philosophy major! She was kind, clearly a loyal friend. Not to mention, she was funny. She made him laugh, even at himself. He'd spent a lifetime taking himself too seriously. Plus, she seemed to intuitively grasp the nature of his family…without criticism.

He shifted in his seat, unsure of what was happening but suspecting he was falling fast. But what was her relationship status? Was there someone in her life? Could that be why she was upset after their earlier encounter?

"So Olivia Keller…do you have a boyfriend in New York or Pittsburgh or some other American city that I probably can't find on a map?"

She smirked. It was not quite a denial. His gut clenched.

"Define 'boyfriend'..." she began. "I thought I had somcthing with a guy. We were in an odd relationship..."

Okay, she referred to the situation in past tense and with a comforting ambivalence. That was good.

"I was seeing him... Sebastian Alexander... doesn't that sound like it should be a fake name? That alone should have been a hint. Anyhow, we'd been on and off, and recently it became more off than on. The final straw was when he decided to go on a Las Vegas boys' trip rather than accompany me to my best friend's wedding. And honestly, my heart checked out long before my head, if my heart was ever involved at all. You know how sometimes you get into something because it's convenient and becomes a habit, but then you set an arbitrary endpoint? That was me getting on the plane to Monaco. I knew the relationship was done."

Nikos understood more than he wanted to admit, especially regarding dead-end relationships. He wished he could explain his life to her. But then he'd have to reveal too much. It wasn't the time. Yet.

"And you?" She eyed him directly. "You aren't seeing anyone?"

"No, no one. Like I told you yesterday, I'm currently quite single." At least that wasn't a lie.

Ironically, in the two days he'd spent with Olivia, she'd seen more of the real Nikos Leonikaros than he shared with anyone. Could she possibly understand that he wasn't trying to be dishonest but was intrigued by the novel sensation of a woman liking him for himself? Not for his money or image?

And when, not if, he confessed all, and if they were somehow to become a couple, could he guarantee Olivia wouldn't take advantage of him? His blood ran cold at the thought. It wasn't an idle fear. Athena had shamelessly milked their relationship for her own profit. Then she'd cheated on him and left him to pay her bills. It was not an experience he ever wanted to repeat, and since then, he'd not let anyone close enough to cause that kind of emotional damage. But now, an urgent voice inside his head insisted that he couldn't let that past drag him down. He had to trust that this American girl might be different.

And hopefully, when he did reveal his true identity, Olivia would recognize his confession as one of those critical junctions she mentioned. Could she appreciate his wealth and the opportunities it represented as another example of her stumbling unintentionally into good fortune? Or would she, too, become blinded by the proximity to status and fame?

"Here's a question...if money were no object, what would you do? Would you still work at your current job?" he asked.

"Oh, *let's pretend* is always an interesting game..." she said, swirling the wine slowly around her glass. "Would I continue to live in a studio apartment smaller than a Monaco hotel room? No, definitely not. Would I stay in New York City? Uncertain. Would I stop working? I probably wouldn't stay at my current job, but I couldn't stand not doing anything. I mean, I may not have a long-term goal, but everyone needs a purpose, right?"

She lifted a brow. "Are you thinking about what you might do next? You said you were facing a big career change."

"I am," he agreed, "but it's more that I want to learn what's important to you. You asked me earlier about traveling. Is that something you would do?"

"Absolutely, yes," she said. "When Maggie and I graduated, we took a ten-day cruise. I think the most magical thing in the world is waking up somewhere you've never been. We splurged and got a room with a balcony. Looking out over the landscape as you arrive at a port in someplace new is the best."

"And what would you do when you got off the boat?" he wondered. "Again, if money were no object."

"Oh, that's easy," she insisted. "I'd visit every museum in the world. Art, history. Cultural sites. I'd see live performances—theater, music, dance, whatever. Explore. The seven wonders of the world. UNESCO heritage sites."

"Not much of a shopper?" he prompted. Athena had maxed out several of his credit cards despite their exorbitant limits.

"It depends," she replied. "I'd hit Paris flea markets hard and buy vintage clothes and antiques to decorate my money-is-no-object mountain chalet. But I don't think I'd splurge on designer clothes."

"A mountain chalet," he repeated. "So, you are a mountain person? Not an ocean person."

"Where I grew up is hilly, so yes, I love the mountains, but I'm sure I could be swayed to favor the sea. You're doing a great job today convincing me. I could adapt." She tilted her head. "And what about you? You obviously like to travel, if the ink on your back is any indication. If money were no object, what would you do differently? Other than expand your already extensive collection of racing paraphernalia."

Oh God, if she had any idea that money really was no object. But her question interrupted the ever-present narrative that most women would exploit his wealth. He turned his thoughts back inward.

What could he be doing that he wasn't already? If he weren't racing, what might he do differently? How would he travel if he could be anonymous in the places he visited?

And what would it be like to travel with Olivia, to roam freely? Explore anonymously? Drink coffee at sidewalk cafés uninterrupted. Take the subway. Sit among the fans at sporting events. Go to a baseball game and see what the American sport was all about.

"I'd eat different foods in all the places I visited. Try all the famous restaurants. Sample all the local specialties. Taste everything. Take cooking classes."

Over-indulging in international cuisine was a plan his nutritionist discouraged.

"Oh, I support that." She smiled. "The food has been the best part of my visit to Monte Carlo so far..." She caught herself and hesitated before she amended her statement. "Other than spending time with you..." She faltered, eyeing him to gauge his reaction. "That's actually been the best and completely unanticipated aspect of my trip."

"Do you mean that?" he asked. His heart skipped an erratic beat.

"I do," she said after the briefest pause. She looked at him intently. "I just don't know what to do about it."

Indeed. They could pretend time would stand still, and they could float along on the brilliant blue sea forever. But in reality, she had a job and a life awaiting her in New York City. He had five more months on his contract. Ten more races. However, after that...could a future exist for them based on a precious few days' worth of encounters? Or did she assume he'd be just a fond memory, a sweet souvenir of Monte Carlo?

Did he want to build a relationship? Was he finally ready to try for something real?

Judging by how his heart leapt at the thought, it was a distinct possibility.

He hesitantly considered certain daydreams that he hadn't allowed himself to imagine for a very long time. What would it be like to sail home to Kallitheira with Olivia at his side?

Oddly, he could see it. She said she liked waking up in unexplored locations. He could make that happen. They could spend the night making love on his favorite secluded island beach and then greet the Aegean dawn. He could imagine her discussing art with his mother or debating business strategy with his father and sisters.

But for the moment, he had more pressing concerns.

The sun spilled molten fire over the edge of the horizon. It was getting late.

"If we are going to stay out all night, I need to move the boat."

She nodded, although it wasn't an unequivocal answer.

"Do you want to stay out?"

"Yes," she said. "I do. I do want to."

Okay. The adventure continued.

He wouldn't assume she was saying yes to resuming their earlier passions. Still uncertain but willing to see how the night might progress, he steered the boat to a sheltered spot a good distance away from their previous anchor spot. He wanted to give her plenty of time to tell him to change course.

She didn't.

He prompted her to tell him more about her childhood. She unselfconsciously complied, painting a place he'd never considered but was now curious about. He noticed she focused on stories of her and her best friend rather than any further mention of her family. He chose not to push her. Apparently, her past was complicated.

When they arrived at his intended destination, he dropped anchor in the rapidly growing dark and set the mandatory night lights.

What next?

"I've got blankets and pillows. Do you want to sleep in the bed on the lower deck or up on the sun pad?" he asked. "Both are comfortable. I could sleep in one place and you in the other…"

"Sleep in different places?" She raised a provocative eyebrow. "What fun would that be? It would defeat the purpose of staying out. Right?"

His mouth went dry. "Would it?"

"Yeah." She stood and moved toward him, her intentions clear. His heart thudded. When the girl made up her mind, apparently, she made up her mind. He admired decisiveness.

"I told you—I think spending time with you is the best thing I've experienced in Monaco so far. But I'm hoping the trip is about to get even better," she murmured.

Okay. The way she said it left little doubt that she was interested in taking their relationship to the next level very soon, if not immediately. He was glad he had optimistically stashed a few condoms. Even so…

What if they did make love? Would she regret it? This time, he wouldn't make any assumptions.

"Are you saying we should continue where we left off this afternoon?"

"Yeah," she murmured. "I behaved weirdly then, but that was my mistake. A mistake I'd like to rectify."

"I don't know if it was a mistake. Maybe just a little uncertainty. But I would like to try again. See what happens between us. I would like that very much. Because I find myself very, very attracted to you."

She took a deep breath and pulled the shirt up over her head.

"Damn." He caught his breath.

She stood, waiting. Not with uncertainty, but it seemed she was simply allowing him the pleasure of looking at her. She unconsciously ran her tongue over her upper lip, not in planned seduction but perhaps in anticipation. He wanted her badly.

"Come here," he gently beckoned.

She stepped closer to where he sat. She stood between his legs and grasped his shoulders. He reached for her hips. They were perfectly designed to fit between his hands. He inhaled the intoxicating scent of skin, sunblock, and salt.

He reverently traced her faded tan lines. As her chest rose and fell, the muscles of her abdomen constricted and jumped. Was it with pleasure? Anticipation? He held her gaze and leaned forward to take her breast into his mouth.

Would her reaction reflect desire or…?

There was no hesitancy. Her eyes grew dark with

need. She twisted her fingers through his hair encouragingly.

"Do you know," she whispered, "I've never had sex outdoors."

He grinned against her skin, allowing wicked thoughts to run wild as he rubbed his cheek in the silken valley of her chest.

"First time on a motorcycle. First time to make love outdoors. I think I am good for you, Olivia Keller," he suggested.

"And how am I good for you, Nikos?" she prompted.

"Oh, you are very good," he growled. "Maybe even perfect."

He nipped her ever so lightly. Her breath caught, and he felt her hips rock beneath his hands.

"Am I the first American girl you've been with?" she asked.

"Yes, but that's the least of it," he admitted distractedly. "I think it might be more than that. Maybe you make me remember things I'd forgotten that I wanted."

"What do you mean?"

He couldn't answer. Wouldn't answer. He was not ready to voice his feelings; they were too raw, made him too vulnerable. Could he trust this intensity? This fervor? Could their unprecedented connection evolve into the kind of relationship he'd longed for but refused to attempt since Athena?

He hooked a finger in one knot of her bikini bottom side strings. "May I?"

She nodded, and he slowly loosened each tie. He spanned her hips and began to ease her clothing down. It slid slowly over the curve of her hips, then dropped rapidly to the floor. She stepped free and stood before him, his own Venus on a half shell, surrounded by gentle waves.

Looking at her, his raw need was demanding and blatant. He made no effort to conceal it; she had to be aware. Olivia coaxed him to stand, then fussed with the drawstring at his waist. He couldn't wait. He shoved his still-tied trunks down and off and kicked them aside.

The moment hung, infinite and incredible. He reveled in the extraordinary sensation of being together, their naked bodies caressed by the salty air, under the darkening sky. He carefully wrapped her in his arms. As her smooth belly brushed against him, he covered her warm mouth with his own, desperate to resume the earth-shattering kisses they shared earlier. His fingers worked through her braided hair. Some loosened and danced around them like a halo.

They stood, kissing, hands stroking, bodies undulating, for as long as he could endure. But she was melting into his arms. He needed to have her, be one with her.

"Do you want to go below deck or stay outside?" he asked.

"Mmm, outside. Under the sky," she purred.

He maneuvered them toward the boat's bow without breaking contact or ceasing his foray of kisses. They stumbled backward onto the sun pad. As they lay down together, he leaned over her, carefully aligning his body alongside hers. He didn't want her to feel trapped, even though he yearned to feel her moving beneath him. Desire flared acute and insistent; he was hard as a marble statue. But he didn't want to rush her; he wanted her invitation. Dear God, she was so beautiful. He could only hold off for so long. He ached for her but wanted her to find pleasure first. He intensified his kisses as he traced his hands over her body. It didn't take long to coax her to peak. He had barely touched her before her face crumpled, and she jammed her fist into her mouth to tamp her cry.

"Olivia," he whispered, nudging his face into her hair. "You don't need to be quiet. There's no one out here but us."

Her eyes stayed closed, but the side of her mouth quirked up in half a smile.

"I'm used to thin apartment walls," she admitted. "You make me feel so good."

"We're not done yet," he said.

"I know." She opened her eyes and lazily rolled toward him. She cradled his cheek. "Just give me a minute and I'll return the favor."

"That's not what I meant," he insisted. If she touched him, the encounter would end in a hot second. "I'm not finished with you yet. Making you feel good."

He demonstrated exactly what he meant.

She gasped and quivered.

"Damn. What did I do to get so lucky?" she managed to ask before he made her moan again.

He chuckled and increased the intensity of his efforts, watching her face and waiting for the delicious moment she lost control.

"I want to hear you cry out," he cajoled as she approached another glorious peak.

As he felt her begin to shudder, to tip over the edge, she called his name.

"Nikos," she insisted. She tugged at him. "Now, I need you now."

Ready to explode at the sound of his name in her mouth, the pleading tone of her voice, and the intensity in her eyes, he reached for the condom packet he'd tucked in the compartment by the sunbed. Once it was secure, he shifted on top of her pliant and receptive body.

"Please, Nikos…"

She snaked her arms around his neck and strained upward to kiss him. Her desire destroyed any shred of restraint or sanity, and he enthusiastically met her demand.

The rhythm of their bodies surged, accentuated by the motion of the boat. Nikos fought valiantly to remain in control but utterly lost himself in the glory of the act. Ensconced in her heat, cocooned in her arms and legs, her gasps ringing in his ears… emotion poured out of him. Words of lust and love spilled out, whispered in Greek. The sensations he experienced were simply too profound to express in anything other than his native language. It didn't matter. He intuitively trusted that she would somehow, miraculously, understand what he meant, how he felt, and how he'd never experienced anything like this before.

His release was immense and encompassed by hers. Even before the last throbbing shudders had subsided, he dropped heavily atop her. She instinctively stroked his back until consciousness returned. He realized he was probably crushing her, so although he didn't want to move, he rolled beside her. She nestled snugly against his chest, and he pulled a blanket over their flushed bodies.

He took a huge gulping breath. What to say after a possibly life-altering experience? Had it been the same for her? Where to even begin?

"That was…" He faltered.

"It was," she whispered, affirming perfectly the indescribable pleasure they'd shared. He grinned and cuddled her a little closer to kiss her shoulder.

"I didn't mean to rush, but it was intense…" he apologized. "Sorry if I went too fast."

Her body started shaking. Was she crying again? Laughing?

"What?"

"That's not what you said about the motorcycle…" She rolled toward him, definitely laughing. "You know I'm joking, right?" She paused. "It wasn't too fast—it was perfect."

He grinned against her hair. He loved that she teased him. She wasn't stupefied in awe of Nikos Leonikaros, celebrity driver. She was affectionately amused by Nikos, just Nikos, and his tendency to go too fast, even when experiences might be better savored.

"It's exactly what I told you about riding the motorcycle..." he insisted. "Hang on tight and let me do the rest."

"I'll keep that in mind for next time."

Next time. She wanted there to be a next time.

Whatever was happening between them, it was accelerating. Rapidly. Should he go flat out or hit the brakes? He'd made mistakes before and paid the price. But being too cautious was also a mistake. He had no idea which way to go. At the moment, he was driving blind.

WEDNESDAY MORNING

OLIVIA BLINKED AS the unflinching Mediterranean morning sun forced her awake. She'd slept like the dead under the infinite sky, in the warm shelter of Nikos's body. He was still unconscious, breathing heavily next to her. She turned over onto her belly and picked up his leaden arm to look at his watch.

"Oh no, no, no, no, no… It's late! I'm going to be so late!" she yelped. She scrambled off the sun pad and snatched up her discarded clothing.

Murmuring in Greek, Nikos rolled into a groggy, half-awake state.

"Damn, damn, damn," Olivia muttered, hopping on one leg to get into her linen pants, giving up on the missing bikini bottoms in the name of dressing expediently. "I'm supposed to be at a gown fitting in less than an hour."

"What time is it…?" Nikos muttered and then groaned. "Oh damn, I'm in trouble."

Apparently, Nikos also had commitments that morning. She had precious little time to relish the sight of his sculpted body in full light as they both hustled to put on the bare minimum of clothing.

Fortunately, there was also no time for any morning-after awkwardness. Always attentive, Nikos offered, and Olivia gratefully accepted, another race-themed garment. As he started the boat and raised the anchor, she pulled on his sweatshirt and tamed her hair under the cap he'd given her the day before.

"Full speed?" he confirmed.

She dropped onto the bench and braced herself. "Full speed."

It wasn't a long trip back to Porte de Fourmis. When they pulled into the slip, Nikos gave precise instructions, and Olivia helped him secure the boat efficiently.

"What about the leftovers from dinner?"

"Leave them."

That was going to be gross, but it wasn't her problem. Hopefully, it wouldn't get him in trouble with the boat's owner.

Nikos set a fast pace. They sprinted up the long dock toward the lot where he'd left his bike the morning before. So much had happened since then; it felt like her entire life had transformed. But she had no time to reflect on it.

Before they donned their helmets, she eyed him squarely. "Nikos."

He looked up, and she thought she saw a hint of wariness at her abrupt tone.

"I can't believe I'm saying this, but I cannot be late for this appointment. We need to get back to

Monte Carlo as quickly as possible. We need to go as fast as you can."

His guarded expression turned into a brilliant smile. "That sounds like my favorite kind of challenge. Are you sure? Because I can go very fast."

"I'm trusting you, but let me tell you, if you get me killed…who is the mythical Greek guy who has to push the boulder up the hill forever?"

"Sisyphus."

"And the guy who gets his liver plucked out by an eagle every day?"

"Prometheus."

"Okay. If you get me killed, I am going to spend eternity haunting your ass so hard that it's going to seem like Sisyphus and Prometheus have it easy in the afterlife."

Undeterred, he took up her hand and kissed it. "Get on. Hang on tight. Let me do the rest."

"Where have I heard that before?" she murmured from the rear seat, giving him an affectionate and trusting squeeze.

Thirty death-defying minutes later, they came to an abrupt stop at the hotel's service entrance. Olivia jerked her helmet off. Nikos removed his as well.

As she started to bolt for the door, he grabbed her arm. "Olivia."

"Yes?" She spun back toward him. "Nikos, I have to go…"

Before she could finish the statement, he pulled her close and kissed her. Hard.

"Olivia. My next few days are complicated. I want to see you again, but we need to talk."

Olivia's stomach instinctively lurched. Those were always dangerous and confusing words. When her father used them—and he had used them a lot—it inevitably meant something bad was going to happen. But she didn't have time to hear what Nikos wanted to discuss. She fought down a flare of panic. Had he not been as profoundly moved by their night together as she had? It was hard to tell during their mad scramble to get back to the hotel.

"Okay, you have my number. Last night was amazing. Text and we'll meet. I still have to get the cookies from you, so I assume I'll see you tomorrow. Right?"

He nodded. Okay, well, that was a good sign.

Olivia glanced up and noticed her reflection in a nearby window. It was rough. "Heh, can I borrow your sunglasses? I'm a hot mess."

"No, you're not. You're gorgeous."

He was still tossing out cheesy lines, which was also good.

"Nikos, please. Just let me borrow your sunglasses. I will give them back..."

"Here, take them. Keep them. And yes, I'll have the cookies for you tomorrow morning."

"You're the best. Really. Thank you for everything."

She crammed the sunglasses onto her face and recklessly kissed him once more before sprinting into the hotel. Whatever he wanted to talk about, a lingering kiss couldn't hurt.

There was no time to stop by her room and pull herself together. As she entered the private wedding salon, she assured herself she could own the superstar-celebrity-sunglasses look. And everybody in Monte Carlo was wearing racing gear. No one could fault her for that.

Maggie and Céline, perfectly attired, waited in the elegant space. It was mortifying.

Céline's eyes widened. Maggie flashed an ornery grin that hadn't changed since she was two years old. Olivia knew she was totally busted.

"Oh, hey, Liv!" Maggie said brightly.

"Mags, I'm so sorry I was running late this morning," Olivia apologized. "Something, er… came up. It took me longer than I thought to get here."

Mags raised her eyebrows knowingly, and Olivia could read every double entendre and innuendo unsaid.

"No problem. Of course we waited for you. Céline, you remember my friend Olivia? My maid of honor?"

Maggie's lips were twitching, and Olivia knew her best friend was suppressing a fit of laughter.

Céline nodded graciously. It was to her credit that she betrayed no disapproving looks. This was the second time she'd seen Olivia in utter disarray.

"Bonjour." The wedding planner poured a cup

of coffee, which Olivia accepted gratefully. Unfortunately, no *pain au chocolat* accompanied it.

Céline turned to Maggie. "Margot, I will go get the gown and the seamstress now that Olivia has arrived."

Olivia could almost hear the silent countdown as the wedding coordinator left the room. The instant the door shut, Maggie pounced.

"Olivia. Keller. Tell me everything, *right now.* When I searched your location this morning, your dot was in the Mediterranean. I guessed you either had a *hot* night with a hot Greek…*or* the guy was psycho and dumped your body at sea. Given that you are not dead *and* you are wearing an interesting mix of purloined race-wear with the clothes you wore yesterday, am I correct in assuming you just did a Monte Carlo walk of shame?"

Maggie should have been a trial lawyer. She knew how to badger a suspect. So many words before Olivia had managed to finish her coffee.

Olivia tried to look innocent. And failed. She couldn't suppress the insanely satisfied grin of a woman who had just crawled back from an earth-shattering night. On a boat. With the sexiest man ever.

"Oh my God, you *did* do a Monte Carlo walk of shame. That is *epic*!" Maggie shrieked. "Liv, I want to be you when I grow up."

"Oh, because Stefano and the Swiss chateau isn't a fairy tale enough?" Olivia retorted good-naturedly. "Margot."

"Margot is my European alter ego," said Maggie primly. "And true, Stefano is too cute to give up. But! Forget my fairy tale. You need to tell all right now. What happened on your magical Mediterranean cruise? You spent the night on the boat with Nikos?"

Olivia could only nod, the color in her cheeks rising.

"So, I'm getting my cookies, and from the way you are blushing, you got a little something sweet, too?" Maggie suggested euphemistically.

Olivia collapsed forward and buried her face in her hands. "Oh my God, Mags, that man made me feel like I have never felt before."

Maggie persisted. "And? Say more. Will you see him again? Is there a possibility for a repeat performance? Damn, Liv, do you even know his last name?"

"Oh Lord, he told me, but he's got about sixteen Greek middle names, so I'm not exactly sure where one name ends and the other begins. Does it matter? And yes, I absolutely need to see him again."

Maggie went wide-eyed. "Seriously?! Do you think it's for real? Like, not a travel fling?"

"I don't know," Olivia moaned. "How can it be for real? He lives here. I live in New York City and I'm leaving on Saturday. And remember, please don't say anything in front of Céline. He works here, and I don't want to get him in trouble."

"Oh, right, right," Maggie agreed. She assumed a mask of innocence as Céline, accompanied by the seamstress, returned with the dress. Momentarily suppressing thoughts of Nikos, Olivia gave her full attention to the maid-of-honor gown. It looked small. Way too small.

In the dressing room, Olivia tried to wriggle her way into the dress. It wasn't going past her hips. She imagined frighteningly large dollar signs to cover the cost of alterations.

"Heh, Liv…these are some serious sunglasses you have here. Expensive ones. Stefano just bought a pair," Maggie commented from beyond the curtain.

"I borrowed them from Nikos," Olivia said. "My boy likes some bling. You should see his watch. I've got to tell him if you're going to wear dupes, at least go for something a little more subtle."

"You aren't going to change his mind on the sunglasses. Every guy in Monaco is wearing this style—real ones and dupes—because one of the F1 drivers always wears them. I don't remember which one. I can't keep up with all the racing divas."

"And people say women are trendy." Olivia snorted.

She tried to ignore a disconcerting ripping noise as she forced her shoulders through the dress.

"I'm struggling. Can you try to zip me?" Olivia poked her head out.

As she'd done with every formal gown Olivia had ever tried on, Maggie joined her in the dressing room and fought with the zipper. Olivia assessed her reflection.

"I may be a hot mess this morning, Mags, but clean hair and makeup will not fix this."

Maggie frowned. "I know, babe. It won't zip. This is not going to work. And by the way, nice hickey on your shoulder. Haven't seen one like that since you were sixteen."

"Shut it, Margaret. But I have an idea," Olivia suggested, seizing on a money-saving possibility. "My suitcase finally arrived. I have a bronze satin Ralph Lauren that I was going to wear for the yacht cocktail party. I got it at a vintage store in Brooklyn for sixty bucks. It's the most gorgeous dress I've ever put on my body. I could wear that. And the dress will conceal the um…yeah, the mark on my shoulder."

Maggie turned decisively to the wedding coordinator. "Céline, can you work bronze into the color scheme?"

Maggie wasn't worried about the expense.

"Oui." The wedding planner made a note. "We will add bronze elements to the flower arrangements and use bronze napkin rings. It will be very elegant."

"I'm going to inspire napkin rings?" Olivia whispered.

Maggie kicked her in the shins. "That sounds perfect. Thank you, Céline."

"That woman has got to hate me," Olivia admitted as the wedding planner left, presumably to round up napkin rings. "Hey Mags…you know how my wedding invitation originally included a plus-one?"

Maggie grinned broadly. "I know what you're about to ask. I should make you beg."

"Nikos is baking a billion cookies for you. I would like to bring him as my date."

Maggie pretended to hesitate, then surrendered to excitement. "Of course! I am dying to meet this guy."

Olivia hugged the incredibly accommodating bride-to-be. "You are the best. I don't know exactly when I'll talk to him next. He had to rush back this morning, so I assume he is working today. And he said those four terrifying words—'We need to talk.' I want to hear what that's all about before I invite him."

"Scary," Maggie agreed. "Honestly, Liv, you can decide at the last minute. It's all good. Céline can squeeze in an extra place setting."

"I'll let you know as soon as I get an answer."

She hugged Maggie again, and then Olivia headed to her hotel room for a long shower and an even longer nap. And to mentally revisit every glorious moment with Nikos.

But as she got onto the elevator, a niggling anxiety rose in her throat. How could she fully enjoy reliving their passionate night when she knew she was boarding a plane for New York in three days?

And since when had she felt any remorse about leaving a travel fling behind? She shivered, afraid to acknowledge the uncharted territory she'd stumbled into.

* * *

After being waylaid by a succession of fans who easily recognized him without his sunglasses, Nikos finally made it back to the team suite.

The troops were marshaled.

"Ya," Nikos met them with a casual Greek greeting.

"Where have you been?" Aleko demanded, responding in Greek.

Nikos ignored him.

"You are late. Really late." Bryson picked up the conversation in English. "You skipped training, which you will regret when that shoulder flares up midway through the race. You have a press conference in fifteen minutes, and there is no way you are going to be on time."

"Then they'll wait," Nikos growled. "Let me get my kit on—give me ten seconds."

Within minutes, they were hustling down the hall. Bryson handed Nikos a bottle of water.

"Your parents and sisters arrive Saturday. I've put them in Hôtel Hermitage…" Bryson commented as they entered the elevator. "You've got the press conference in ten minutes. After that, you've got the pit walk. Then the crew needs you in the garage to check the seat fitting." He swiped his iPad. "The Monaco commemorative helmet and suit will be unveiled this afternoon. They want photos. And Eero wants an extra strategy session to make sure it's a Segno Rosso double podium. I can try to work in another massage for the shoulder."

"Eero's strategy better involve Juan-Carlos keeping his head and doing his job," Nikos muttered, referring to the team principal and Nikos's rookie teammate. Mentoring the kid made Nikos feel like an old man. He'd once been that raw, that talented, and that undisciplined. But racing had been exhilarating back then. Now the exhilaration he felt resulted not from the possibility of a podium but the possibility of spending more time with an incredible woman. What an unbelievable night it had been. But could it become an ongoing thing? Could he handle a true relationship? What if it went all south? Last time, relationship trauma had nearly ended his career. Now, when he was so close to achieving his final major racing goal, was it wise to allow himself to become distracted?

He didn't bother protesting as they took Bryson's preferred exit route through the main lobby, but Nikos ignored all autograph requests. He usually wasn't blatantly rude to fans, but the clock was ticking. It was bad enough facing the scrum of reporters at the mandatory press conference, let alone arriving late.

A courtesy car waited outside the hotel. Aleko cut through the gathered crowd. As he opened the door for Nikos, he turned to Bryson. "I need a word with him. Get in the front."

Nikos was definitely in for it. Then again, how much grief could the old man heap on him in the five-minute drive to the media center?

Aleko eyed Nikos. "What the hell are you doing?" he demanded in Greek.

"What do you mean?" Nikos answered in English.

"With this girl. What are you doing?"

Nikos was getting irritated. He switched over to Greek. "None of your damn business."

"Nikolaes, it is my business." When Aleko used his full name, Nikos knew the man was about to get heavy. But Nikos wasn't a child. He wasn't a shy first-year driver overwhelmed by newfound celebrity. He didn't need a babysitter. He had no patience for lectures from his long-time minder.

"What is my job? What has always been my job?"

"Don't be vague, Aleko," Nikos ground out. "Say what you're going to say. Better yet, just shut the hell up."

"What is my job?" he repeated.

"Damn it, Aleko. I don't know."

"You do know!" the old man exploded. "It's to keep you safe! It's always been to keep you safe. That's it. That's my job." He paused for effect. "And right now, you aren't safe. Think about how things went with…with you know who."

Aleko wouldn't even say Athena's name.

"For God's sake…"

But Aleko wasn't done.

"You're distracted. You're not focused on the race, and you know it. This is how drivers get hurt. Think, Nikolaes! This is why you don't date during the season. You need a woman? Bryson has plenty of women who want to meet you. You have dinner. You take her back to your room. Easy. Done."

"Stop. You need to stop right there. It's offensive."

"You don't go sailing off and spend the night on the damn boat! You don't get moony over a nobody American girl and walk around with your head up your ass! This will not end well, Nikolaes. You are living dangerously. And I can't let you do that."

"How are you going to stop me?" Nikos opened the car door and prepared to brave the gauntlet of photographers surrounding the media center. He turned back to Aleko. "I don't know how you think you can stop me, but I'm telling you right now—do not cross me on this, Aleko. Do. Not."

With that, Nikos kicked the door shut and steeled himself for a day of forced conviviality. He would endure it so he could win one more time at Monaco.

Late that night, after the rehearsal dinner, Olivia lay drowsily in bed, staring at her phone's wan glow. Monte Carlo was blanketed in serene silence, but a raging mental debate kept her awake.

Should she text? It had been exactly twenty-four hours since they'd made love. Less time since she'd kissed him goodbye in the alleyway. By her usual timeline, it was way too soon to text. In New York, she'd give a guy she'd hooked up with at least a week. She was no clinging vine. And when she did check in, she always kept the tone light and the expectations low. But now she didn't have unlimited time to see how things would play out. Nikos was a craving she couldn't ignore, like knowing she had peanut butter–chip ice cream in the freezer. She couldn't hold off for twenty-four hours, let alone a week. But would her eagerness scare him? She was used to pushing guys away, not reeling them in!

As she deliberated, her phone lit up; it was a text from Nikos.

Olivia let out a massive sigh of relief. Okay, she could still steer this boat. She didn't have to act like she'd lost her mind. Even if maybe, she had.

I've been thinking about you all day

Oh yeah? What have you been thinking?

Can't say—phone would explode, thoughts are too hot...

She blushed from head to toe with pleasure. His next text appeared before she could respond.

...was that cheesy?

Absolutely. But very appreciated and reciprocated

Any chance I might see you again? Not just for hot stuff

Olivia shrieked out loud, thankful she was alone.

I'd like that—and hot stuff would be fun—just saying

Anything you want. When?

Was asking him to be her plus-one for the wedding be too much? She wavered. Maybe he wasn't available; she didn't know his work schedule. Olivia didn't want to take a big, vulnerable risk if his attendance wasn't even possible.

Maybe see you tomorrow? What's your schedule?

I'll check and text you in the AM

Okay. She'd hold off on the big ask until then.

Apparently, she wasn't the only one eager for this, whatever it was, to continue.

Sounds good...

...Good night Nikos

Kalinixta, Olivia

THURSDAY MORNING—WEDDING DAY

OLIVIA BASKED IN another glorious Mediterranean sunrise. She had awoken in a state of euphoria. It was going to be a fantastic day. Her best friend was getting married. And Olivia was head over heels for her own guy, who was surely evidence that magic existed in the world. Life was good. So good. Maybe it would only last for another day or two…maybe once the pixie dust cleared, she'd be back to her ho-hum reality, but in the beautiful sun-drenched morning, she didn't care. She'd enjoy it while it lasted.

While simultaneously drying her hair and dancing around with pent-up joy, there was a knock on her hotel room door. She paused her music and pulled on the hotel bathrobe, thinking there was nothing so luxurious as a plush, complimentary robe.

In the hall, a uniformed attendant revealed a cart piled high with wide, shallow cardboard bakery boxes.

"*Madame.*" He nodded. "I am to deliver these to you."

Olivia waited while he stacked the boxes on the credenza. Nikos was such a gem. A keeper. What man would bake wedding cookies for someone who had been a perfect stranger only thirty-six hours earlier?

Well. They certainly weren't strangers anymore. An infusion of heat stirred Olivia's entire body, remembering their time on the boat. Damn, her knees literally went weak. How soon could she see him again? Would he agree to be her last-minute date for the wedding? She pictured his appreciative look when he saw her in the bronze gown. Her fantasy morphed to imagining them dancing together at the reception…and then returning to her hotel room where he could take off her dress and treat her to another round of indulgent lovemaking. It was almost too much to contemplate. She felt like she might explode out of her skin.

She had no sooner picked up her hair dryer again than her phone buzzed. Speak of the devil.

Did cookies arrive?

YES so amazing! they look delicious thank you…

…I can't even tell you how happy you've made me

She didn't care. She was utterly shameless at this

point, rapid-fire texting. She wanted him again. Badly.

I'd rather show you my appreciation—you around?

There was a longer pause than Olivia would have liked.

Finishing up at the gym—could stop briefly before work

How briefly? you like to go fast. just saying

Be there in 5

When he knocked approximately three minutes later, Olivia threw the door open to discover Nikos, glistening with sweat, his hair damp under his hoodie. The evidence of his workout only made him more appealing as he flashed that devastating smile she'd been dreaming of. Good Lord, she wanted to devour him.

"Did you run all the way here?"

"Figured I'd extend the workout."

Olivia bit her tongue. Oh, she had plans to extend his workout. "Come on in…"

He noticed the towering boxes and lifted the lid of the top one. "Are the cookies good?"

Why would he doubt it?

"The cookies are exactly what I needed, what

Maggie wanted. You don't even understand how important this is."

He smiled again with such sweetness that it made her ache. "It wasn't a big deal."

Olivia had to correct that perception. "Nikos, it is a big deal. Like me, Maggie was raised by a single mom. Her mom and grandma died before she graduated. They never got to celebrate her international internship. They never got to meet her fiancé. They couldn't imagine her living this crazy, glamorous life." Olivia paused, taking a moment to compose her emotions. "The cookies are the connection to people from her childhood, like me. That's important to me. I can't afford to give Maggie an expensive gift, but this means so much more. It's what is truly important. Does that make sense? You made this possible."

He swallowed. "I had no idea," he admitted. "And I admit I did it for selfish reasons. You see, this incredible girl knocked me off my feet, and I had to convince her to get to know me..."

She rolled her eyes.

"Too cheesy again?"

"Cheesy but effective." Olivia smiled, moved closer, and placed her hands on his warm chest.

His eyes darkened with desire. "I don't know if you want to get too close—I just came from the gym..." He made an unconvincing attempt to warn her off.

She ignored his warning and pulled him into a demanding kiss.

While their previous physical encounter had been framed in uncertainty, this time it was obvious that they both agreed exactly where they wanted to go, even if they didn't have much time to get there.

The belt came undone, and her robe gaped open.

"Oh my God," Nikos murmured, sliding his hands under the garment in appreciation of her naked body. "You smell so good."

"Fancy hotel shampoo," she admitted.

He buried his face in her neck, his hands roving, pulling her closer.

She peeled the damp sweatshirt over his head. He nudged off his running shoes as she backed him toward her still-unmade bed.

"I should maybe put the Do Not Disturb on the door…" she murmured as he slid the robe off her shoulders.

"They'll knock…"

He dropped his running shorts and collapsed like a fallen angel onto the bed.

She waited, wanting to hear his sultry voice issue an invitation once again.

"Come here," he whispered. God, she loved those words when he said them.

Tossing her hair over her shoulder, Olivia settled astride his gloriously chiseled body. Eyes locked with his, she leaned forward and snagged a condom she'd strategically placed on the nightstand.

"Looks like I've got you right where I want you,"

she murmured. "Maybe it's your turn to hang on and let me drive."

From the fervent look on his face, he required no convincing. "I yield."

She rubbed against him, watching the tremors of pleasure play across his face. Finally, sensing that she'd tormented him enough, she ripped the foil packet open and rolled the condom over him. Holding his smoldering gaze, she sank down and reveled in his groan of pleasure.

Moving her hips ever so slightly, she leaned forward, her hair a curtain around his face. She touched her forehead to his. As he brought his mouth onto her skin, she whispered, "Is this going to be a fast or slow ride?"

She felt him smile against her chest. "Whatever you like—you're the driver..."

But despite her intent to prolong their encounter, her body had other ideas. His hands gripped and squeezed as she picked up the pace. Gasping for breath, just when she thought they both were at the point of no return, he abruptly lifted her off his body. She was momentarily confused until she felt him slide down beneath her. Every nerve ending in her body tingled in anticipation. Gripping her hips, he pulled her onto his scalding mouth. If she had thought he was masterful at pleasing her with his fingers, it was nothing compared to what he did with his tongue.

Relentless, he teased her until she absolutely combusted. But before she could collapse boneless onto the bed, he knelt behind her. With her head cradled in her arms on the pillow, she was too raw to do anything but open herself to him. He drove home, the connection pushing her beyond any pleasure she'd ever known. She was coherent of nothing but the sensation of his body filling hers.

"Nikos."

Between gasps, she pleadingly whispered his name. She wasn't sure she could withstand the building crescendo. But she did. And when she shattered for a second time, he exploded with her. He clutched her tightly, and together, they trembled.

As the sensation faded, he collapsed, depleted, along her back and with unintelligible murmurs of satisfaction, dropped sideways, taking her with him. Nikos held her, spooned from nape to thighs. He sighed.

"This wasn't… I mean… I know my text…and your text said…" he murmured.

"What?" she wondered. "What are you trying to say?"

"I wanted to make sure you liked the cookies. I wanted to see you. I didn't come to your room just for this."

"I hope you still managed to enjoy it."

He snorted into her hair. "That's putting it mildly. Good God."

They lay in silence, facing the window, the sparkling vista of Monte Carlo sprawled below them. Olivia swallowed hard. Their lovemaking, whatever physical magic was happening between them, was extraordinary. Unprecedented. Normally, she'd be content with that alone, thrilled by it. But now, wrapped in Nikos's arms, she had a sudden gut-clenching epiphany. She, Olivia Keller, wanted more from him. His sweet words delighted rather than horrified her. Now her biggest terror was knowing her involvement with Nikos would come to a crashing end the moment she stepped on the plane to New York. How was she going to bear it?

Somehow, without realizing it, she'd let this beautiful, kind, and glorious man slip under her well-honed defenses. She suspected this was how people fell in love. Unbelievably, she realized she might be ready for it.

"Yesterday morning, you said we needed to talk," Olivia prompted. She now felt confident enough to ask. Unlike her father, she couldn't believe Nikos would let her down. "Should I ask what you wanted to talk about?"

Before he could reply, Nikos heard his phone buzz. He rolled away from Olivia's delectable body and leaned precariously over the edge of the bed, trying to reach his discarded shorts. No luck. He swung his legs to the floor and rooted through their clothing to locate the phone. It was Bryson.

"Ya."

"Where are you? You said you'd be back from the gym thirty minutes ago. Eero wants you on the portable driving SIM to review the team's final adjustments to the car before you do the track walk.

And I've got new content assignments. And we've got the sponsor reception this afternoon. You've got to get over here. Aleko is losing it."

"Good to know," Nikos murmured, standing naked in front of the window. He'd briefly slipped his handlers, but three days before a race, every movement he made was part of a carefully orchestrated and scheduled preparation. On the streets below, he could see the temporary race structures swarming with people, a hive of industrious bees, all doing their part. He should feel guilty for shrugging off his responsibilities, but somehow, he didn't.

"I'll be there shortly. Tell Aleko to relax."

This was likely one of the few times he'd be able to steal a few moments with Olivia before she left. He'd already concluded he wanted to pursue a relationship that went beyond their sizzling physical encounters. Her impassioned explanation of why the cookies were so important only confirmed his decision.

Unfortunately, there simply wasn't enough time to confess and explain his identity.

She appeared to have absolutely no clue that he wasn't a hotel employee. However, pre-race hoopla was escalating to the point that it would be impossible to ignore. Would she connect the dots? Or would she remain oblivious until he had sufficient time to explain? When she called him to her room, he had planned to tell her the truth. But then her robe gaped open…and coherent thought had flown out of his head.

Now his obligations demanded him. He didn't have time to drop any bombshells. He could only hope the wedding would keep Olivia distracted until he could carve out another hour with her to come clean. But when might that occur?

He turned to her, her skin elegant against the stark white sheets.

"About what I said yesterday, that we needed to talk…"

She rolled over and gave him a questioning look. Frustration gripped him. An insistent voice in his head argued that he just tell her, timing be damned. But it would be messy.

He concentrated on reclaiming his clothing and dressing, not looking at her until he was ready to speak. But what exactly should he say?

She interrupted his thoughts. "Would you want to come to Maggie's wedding with me this afternoon?"

The invitation surprised him.

"It's just that…" he began. "You need to understand…the next few days…"

He looked up, trying to mask his bittersweet disappointment. But when he saw her stricken look, he realized she misunderstood.

Her innocent invitation was so far beyond the realm of possibility—and exactly why it was time for him to be done with racing. He needed to reclaim his life so that when a charming woman asked him to accompany her to an important event, he could do so. And maybe someday he could attend without anyone staring or interrupting to ask for an autograph. His refusal was not about her.

"I'd love to. Really. I'd love to go with you. It would be great to meet your friend and see the cookie display..."

"But?" She sighed. "This is obviously a no."

"I can't," he said, willing her to believe he truly regretted refusing. "I have to work. The next few days are insane."

She sighed while he tied his shoes. "Yeah, I get it. I'm sure with the race coming up, you're slammed."

For a moment, he panicked, but then it made sense. Right. She thought he worked at the hotel. Indeed, the Grand Prix did increase demands on the hotel staff.

But he wasn't on the staff. He was an F1 driver with contractual obligations. He had to be realistic. Before the race, there was no way he could carve out time to do justice to the conversation they needed to have. It was ridiculous to imagine it. His hands were tied. All he could do was hope she didn't stumble onto the truth. But maybe she might stick around a little longer. Was that too much to ask?

"Any chance you might delay your departure for a day?" he suggested. "I will be free Sunday night. It will be late, but we could have dinner. Maybe decide when we might see each other again. If you want to see me again. Because I definitely want to keep seeing you."

There. He'd said it.

Her face fell. "Nikos, by Sunday night, I will be back in New York to go to work on Monday. I'm leaving Saturday."

His gut clenched. "There is no way you might…"

He caught himself. Reality hit hard. What was he asking her to do? Reorder her life? For what? To share one more night so he could confess…and then fly to Spain for the next race? And onto the Segno Rosso headquarters in Italy? Then Montreal. Followed by a tour of cities across the world. He wouldn't be free until mid-December. How could he ask her to do what he could not?

"Olivia…"

She got up, retrieved the discarded bathrobe, and sank into the chair in front of the window. She crossed her legs, ankle hooked behind her calf, and folded her arms protectively.

"I guess this is the problem with travel flings, huh?" Glancing out the window, she looked like she was trying to play it cool and nonchalant, but he suspected it was a facade.

That nearly broke him. He couldn't leave her with the wrong impression. "I don't think of this as a fling. Whatever is happening between us, this isn't a fling."

His phone buzzed again. He ignored it, but she noticed.

"Okay, okay. I understand you need to go. People want you."

"Yeah."

"Nikos..." she blurted. "I am here until Saturday. If you have any time at all, I'd love the chance to get together again."

Okay. Somehow, despite the inconvenience, he had to make it happen. Even if he had to track her down in the wee hours after the wedding, when he probably should be sleeping. He couldn't just let it go. Couldn't just let her go.

"I would love to see you again, too. And it doesn't have to involve sex," he said.

She grinned slyly. "I don't know. The sex is pretty great, so why not take advantage of it while we can? As for long distance, we can figure it out as we go along. If that's what you want."

Long distance? As they went along? She also wanted this to continue?

"I do want to. I really do. What did you call it? Fly by the seat of our pants?"

She smiled brilliantly. "Exactly."

Desire flared once again. He was still savoring the taste of her. God, if he had even another half an hour to spare, he would take her right back to that disheveled bed and prove that his interest would last beyond the weekend, beyond the end of the season. If they could just figure out how to make it work until then.

"I would be thrilled to spend more time with you

while you're here. Doing whatever you'd like to do. I'll see what I can work out."

She flashed him an endearing grin.

But he had dallied long enough. He didn't want to say goodbye, so he hovered, leaning over her chair, capturing her between his arms. Her gold-flecked gaze held his, straightforward and clear. How would those luminous eyes regard him when she knew the truth?

"I meant what I said about my contract being up in December. I could come to New York."

Her body softened, and she blushed, almost shyly. She was many things, this woman, but he didn't think shy was part of her equation.

"You do understand that I live in a tiny studio apartment. Smaller than this hotel room. You'd have to stay very, very close to me." She turned her obvious embarrassment about her small apartment into a flirtatious invitation.

"I would be delighted," he murmured before kissing her, sweet and tender. He made a mental note to tell Bryson to look at property in New York City.

He allowed himself one more kiss and then left her, the door clicking softly behind him.

He showered, dressed, and then endured Bryson and Aleko's directives. But all the while, his thoughts were full of Olivia, the sun catching her hair when they were out on the water. The noises she made when he moved in her body. The frank appreciation she'd shown for their physical encounters. The implication that she might want their relationship to extend beyond a short-term fling.

Something had changed in him the moment he met her. Some switch had flipped. Her appreciation for his help in procuring the cookies had clinched it. It wasn't about his money. He'd help her create something that, by her own admission, money couldn't buy.

Now, for the first time in a very long time, he was tempted to build a relationship that wasn't about convenience or proximity because a relationship with Olivia Keller offered neither. But it might be something real.

However, as the courtesy car transported him through the crowded streets, his confidence began to unravel. He should have found the time to tell her the truth. Could they sustain a relationship once she knew the truth? And would it be worth the effort? For that matter, was there something truly special about Olivia, or was he reacting so powerfully to her merely because the end of his career loomed? Had she simply shown up at a vulnerable moment? He didn't think so. Intuitively, he recognized something unique about her and what they might share. But how could he be sure? He'd misjudged a woman before and been nearly destroyed in the process. The transition out of racing was going to be difficult enough—would it help or hurt trying to simultaneously build a relationship?

As he walked toward the paddock, he wondered,

could a relationship ever be more important than racing?

That astounding thought stopped him dead in his tracks. Literally.

Reality kicked in. What the hell was he thinking?

By standing still, he encouraged the fans who called his name and held their phones to record his approach. He needed to keep moving. At the moment, he was still a driver. He was still very much a part of the show.

The situation with Olivia was a lot to consider. He wanted it—damn, he wanted it—but maybe it was all too much, too soon? He ran his hand through his hair without thinking. The female fans staring at him gave a collective sigh, a thousand camera lenses clicked, and he knew his mindless gesture would be featured on a million social media accounts within moments.

Could he balance the current realities of his very public life on the racing circuit with building a private long-term, long-distance relationship? And what would Olivia make of all this anyhow? Could she handle it?

Almost without realizing it, he had arrived at the Segno Rosso headquarters. He took a deep breath. The familiar, managed chaos of the garage and team center, where everyone was intent on their pre-race preparations, immediately consoled him and brought him back into focus. His spiraling thoughts slammed to a halt as abruptly as a race coming under a red flag.

What was he doing? Why was he focused on five months in the future? Nothing good happened when he got too far ahead of himself. He'd always raced one segment, one turn, one straightaway at a time. Not getting sidetracked had served him well.

Nikos took a deep breath. Maybe Aleko was right. Tying himself in knots before a race, being so distracted…this was dangerous. It wasn't smart. It wasn't fair to his team. People relied on him. Eero, Juan-Carlos. The Segno Rosso engineers and mechanics. The pit crew. His trainers and nutritionists. The marketing team. The sponsors. The fans. Bryson and Aleko, for all that they put up with him. All these people, right here, right now, weighed against a nebulous possibility with a girl who intrigued him but whom he barely knew.

She was leaving on Saturday. She'd mentioned staying connected long-distance, but that might be unrealistically well-intentioned. She might get back home and rekindle with her New York boyfriend, flick the off switch back on. There was no way to predict the future. His best approach would be to give his all to winning the Monaco race and nailing the remainder of the season. Until then, he had to hold off thinking about Olivia Keller, no matter how earth-shattering their connection. Come December, if she was still interested, he could refocus on how a potential relationship could fit into his new life. Whatever that was.

Willing himself to jam his emotions into a tight mental box, Nikos drew upon the discipline he'd cultivated over his long career. He had a job to do, in this moment, in this race. Fantasizing about the next chapter would get him nowhere. Olivia, enticing as she was, would have to wait. He had Media Day and a race to prepare for.

Maggie and Stefano's afternoon wedding was stunningly elegant. It was everything Olivia wanted for her dearest friend. And while having Nikos at her side would have been a pleasure, focusing exclusively on Maggie was also a gift. Still, Olivia hoped there would be at least one more chance to see Nikos before she got on the plane for New York. And after that? Who knew? Their conversation that morning hinted at an unanticipated and tempting future.

When the ceremony concluded, the guests mingled in the ornate gilt ballroom. Olivia joined Maggie, Stefano, and his family for photos as the ever-organized Céline moved them from one spectacular hotel setting to another.

"We need to go to the patio right now," the wedding coordinator insisted. "There is a Formula 1 reception that will take place there shortly. We only have a few minutes before the patio is closed off."

Olivia trotted after the bride, carrying both of their bouquets. Céline, working from her notebook, directed the photographer in rapid French. Maggie and Stefano were instructed to pose for a series of shots by the palms with Monte Carlo as the photogenic background. The newlyweds didn't seem to notice the scenery, however. They were in post-nuptial bliss, positively glowing with love. It was adorable.

Olivia stood with Uncle Klaus and Aunt Kiki, waiting patiently to be summoned for their assigned photos.

"The cookies were such a fabulous touch!" Aunt Kiki whispered to Olivia. "Such a unique tradition. Margot was so appreciative that you would go to such lengths."

"I love Maggie. I'd do anything for her. And I had help with the cookies," Olivia admitted.

Olivia found herself unexpectedly emotional at the heartfelt compliment and the thought of the person who had made the cookie table possible. Weddings made one sentimental, she supposed. It was astounding to recognize that her overflowing feelings weren't only because Nikos physically set her aflame. He also tempted her to rethink longstanding doubts about walking down the aisle. It was hard to believe a whirlwind connection could provoke such desires, but there she was, contemplating a real relationship. Falling in love. Being vulnerable. Trusting someone with her whole heart. She'd never imagined any of these things for herself.

Although she and Maggie had planned their nuptial celebrations from the time they were little girls, those childish plans had focused on the accoutrements of the day—the gowns, the menus, the decor. Their prospective grooms had been vague: tuxedo-clad mysteries overshadowed by other more vividly imagined details. But now, watching Maggie and her husband—husband!—kiss and laugh, Olivia felt an aching sense of nostalgia. Somehow, meeting Nikos and witnessing Maggie and Stefano's wedding resurrected those innocent and long-buried girlhood dreams.

When had Olivia stopped dreaming of a happily-ever-after? That was easy. Probably the umpteenth time her father let her down. Left her and her mother to their own devices; left them to muddle through, terrified they couldn't keep their heads above water. Claimed he couldn't afford to support either of them when, in fact, he was lavishing gifts on a steady stream of mistresses. Olivia had learned to assume that every word out of the man's mouth was likely a lie. Because it was. You couldn't lie your way into a happily-ever-after, so Olivia had been convinced that happily-ever-after didn't exist.

Not surprisingly, she'd had been forced to rely on herself. Not expect help from anyone. And she'd done fine. Not quite happily-ever-after, but fine. Sufficient.

Until Nikos.

Olivia had never met a guy who would selflessly care for her like he did. Her relationships had been with guys who, by mutual agreement, stayed at arm's length. They respected her independence… but they couldn't be bothered to go out of their way for her. Everyone assumed that both parties would benefit from firm boundaries. They were very cognizant of the danger of becoming too reliant on one another. That was how relationships went, right?

Olivia certainly had never expected a guy to show the same kind of reciprocal selflessness she and Maggie shared in their longstanding friendship. She had never met a guy she could imagine capable of a similar unwavering commitment.

Until Nikos.

As a perfect stranger, he had patiently escorted her all over town and asked nothing in return except a tolerance for high speed. He had stayed up all night baking cookies for people he'd never met. He had asked questions and then listened—really listened!—to her answers. He responded to her cues as their physical relationship unfolded. As a lover, he proved generous and passionate…no, he was downright extraordinary. In the whirlwind days they'd spent together, Nikos embodied the kind of man she hadn't known existed. Unbelievably, she might even be falling in love with him.

But she had to leave in thirty-six hours. Was she crazy to get on the plane?

What if she didn't leave? Would she be crazy to stay?

He'd ask if she might delay her departure. Changing her flight based on a guy she'd only met would be a major leap of faith. Not to mention insanely expensive. But December was a long time to wait to see him again. A lot could happen before December. He could forget all about her.

Olivia grappled with her churning, conflicting

instincts. Should she go all in or keep her guard up and expectations low?

"We're going to have to wrap this up. We can finish pictures in the ballroom," Céline said, interrupting Olivia's thoughts. Maintenance workers had arrived with a cherry picker, which they maneuvered next to one of the light poles. As they worked to secure a rolled-up banner, Olivia noticed other people entering the patio.

She took Maggie's bouquet and followed the wedding coordinator toward the oncoming group.

Olivia glanced up…and did a double take. Nikos was one of the people walking toward her. It was as if her fond thoughts had conjured him. She felt a rush of warmth. She really might be falling in love with him. She'd never felt so energized by a mere glimpse of someone. He was unique.

"Nikos!" she called, smiling and waving the flowers jubilantly overhead.

He looked up at the sound of her voice. Even though his eyes were hidden by sunglasses, she was sure she saw pleasure on his face. It delighted her. Perhaps she could take a quick moment and introduce him to Maggie. Would it be premature to introduce him as her boyfriend? She flushed at the thought of it.

But as she opened her mouth to call the bride, Nikos's expression changed. Now his face reflected some other emotion Olivia couldn't quite decode…

"My goodness!" exclaimed Uncle Klaus. "That's

Nikos Leonikaros! And I thought you weren't a racing fan!"

"What?" Olivia asked stupidly. "Who?"

Three things happened at once.

One: A gaggle of women—racing fans, based on their apparel—burst forth from a side door and sprinted toward Nikos, two security guards in pursuit.

Two: The men who had been in the service corridor where she first met Nikos—the burly old man and the smooth talker—flanked Nikos protectively on either side, shielding him from the women headed his way.

Three: The workers on the cherry picker unfurled a gigantic banner. Astoundingly, it depicted… Nikos. But in the picture, he was wearing a red Segno Rosso racing suit and holding a helmet. Number 19.

It made no sense. None of it made any sense.

Olivia stood frozen, dumbly, trying to process what she was seeing.

The security guards intercepted the rowdy fans and steered them back toward the hotel.

Céline murmured apologetically and gestured for the wedding party to make themselves scarce. Quickly. The family complied, even though Uncle Klaus kept sneaking curious glances.

Olivia remained rooted to the spot, her eyes locked on Nikos's inscrutable face. He, too, seemed incapable of movement.

What the hell was going on?

The workers unrolled more banners featuring different F1 drivers. Why was Nikos depicted as one of them?

What. The. Hell?

Olivia's mind turned slowly, replaying her interactions with him over the past few days. The vagueness about his job. The high-speed bike ride. The avoidance of crowds. The expensive sunglasses. She'd been so focused on their intense connection, she hadn't noticed that his story didn't quite add up. Some profound realization nibbled at the edge of her consciousness.

She heard someone else calling his name, demanding an autograph.

Who would want the autograph of a hotel baker?

Surely he hadn't been misrepresenting himself the whole time…surely not. He said he was a baker, not an F1 driver. Right?

The thirty-foot banner strongly suggested otherwise.

Olivia gasped with sudden comprehension.

With picture-perfect slow-motion clarity, in her mind's eye, she saw him on the boat, stripping off his shirt. His beautiful back with its many tattoos. So many racetrack tattoos. Every single one with a date.

The date he won each race.

Everything clicked into place.

Good God.

The utterly unbelievable truth could not be denied. She'd been a total idiot. How had she not seen it?

She clutched her fists against her gut. It was good that she'd eaten very little that day; otherwise, she would have puked on the spot. She could barely breathe. She could barely see. But she'd be damned before she keeled over, damned before she let him drift away in his sea of lies. Blindly, Olivia stormed in his direction.

"Olivia!" Céline cried out. "Please, come this way..."

She ignored the wedding coordinator. "Get out of my way."

"No, no, not here, you cannot talk to him here..." said the burly man in a heavy Greek accent.

The bodyguard moved to block her. She scowled, determined to come face-to-face with Nikos, who had obviously prevaricated from the moment they'd met. He was as big a liar as her father. Maybe bigger. The biggest liar she'd ever met. And that was saying something.

Damn it, how had she been so stupid, stupid, stupid? She knew better than to trust a man. Any man. Especially one who had appeared too good to be true.

"Give us a minute..." she heard Nikos insist as he turned in her direction.

He grimaced in either guilt or shock; Olivia wasn't sure which. But she had no sympathy for whatever he was feeling. Liars never wanted to deal with the consequences of their lies. She'd learned that the hard way, and she wasn't going to let him off the hook. Her father had tried to worm his way back into her good graces, only to lie again. Lies begat more lies. Not a chance she'd allow Nikos to lie to her again. Ever.

The older man refused to budge, so Olivia tried to circumvent him. He placed a restraining hand on her arm. It was a mistake.

"Aleko!" Nikos warned.

Olivia lived in New York City. No one touched her without her permission.

"Get. Your. Hand. Off. Me. *Now*," she growled. Loudly.

"Aleko!" Nikos repeated. He felt utterly helpless as the situation devolved into chaos. "Let her *go*!"

Aleko relented. Olivia thrust her face close to Nikos's. She was frighteningly, blisteringly angry. Rage emanated from her entire body. He could see it in every pore.

"I can explain. Please let me explain." He tried to forestall whatever she was about to say. Of course, her accusations would all be true. He couldn't deny any of it. His gut roiled with guilt.

"Nikos! I do not understand!" Olivia hissed. "Who the hell are you?"

"It doesn't matter. It changes nothing between us. Nothing changes," he desperately pleaded. "I wanted to tell you. Let's take this someplace else…"

"What are you talking about? It changes everything!"

Nikos foolishly attempted to touch Olivia's arm. She shrugged him off as violently as she'd shaken off Aleko.

Yet another group of fans managed to get past the overwhelmed security guards and surged toward them, but Olivia stubbornly held her ground.

He broke into a sickening, ice-cold sweat. Dear God, he needed her to move, to take this conversation somewhere, anywhere, else. Why wouldn't she move? Didn't she understand they could not have this confrontation publicly? He knew the social media storm that would ensue. He'd been forced to weather that kind of grotesque exposure before and would not do it again. Ever. For anyone.

"What the hell is going on?" she ground out through gritted teeth. "Tell me who you really are!"

The answer was as blatant as the gigantic banner and the Segno Rosso faithful clamoring for his attention. Calling his name. Demanding autographs.

Nikos's stomach clenched as he leaned closer to Olivia. He dropped his voice so only she could hear. Her breath was heartbreakingly warm, but he felt like he'd taken a knife to the chest. How had it come to this?

The answer was obvious. He'd been a fool. He should have found the time to explain. He never should have let the ruse go so far. How had he imagined he could fly under the radar in Monaco, of all places? On a race weekend? There had to be a trophy for that kind of wishful thinking, that kind of hubris.

"Please let me explain."

"You lied to me," she seethed. "I cannot, will not deal with men who lie."

"Olivia..."

"A hotel baker?"

He froze, guilty as charged. What was there to say?

"Simple question—is that you on that banner? Yes or no?"

"Yes."

"So, you lied to me. Say it to my face. Say it. Take off your sunglasses, look me in the eyes, and say, 'I am a liar.'"

Keenly aware of the fans closing in, Nikos felt a molten core of anger building at her demand. Why? Why was this happening? Again. With Olivia, he'd hoped to avoid the ravenous public consumption of his most intimate experiences. Yet here was an explosive confrontation. Like Athena all over again. He was blindsided by shame and frustration, spilling out for everyone to witness. Was privacy too much to ask? Of anyone? Ever? And why couldn't Olivia listen to him for two seconds? Could she not grasp that his ruse wasn't intended to hurt her? It was a white lie that, if anything, had allowed them to get to know each other better. If they could just get off the damn patio, he could explain. Or was she reveling in this public smackdown, just like Athena?

He squeezed his eyes shut, trying to find some internal peace and sanity. But for that, he needed to escape the tumult. The intrusiveness of the fans, the incessant video recording and photo taking, Aleko's shouts, the fury in Olivia's face, the hovering sponsors… Nikos wanted to wrap his arms over his head and howl.

He was at the end of his rope. He had to get off the patio immediately, away from salacious onlookers. Away from the rabid audience. Even if Olivia refused.

He made one last attempt. "Olivia, please. We cannot have this conversation here. There are too many fans around."

She inhaled a sharp breath, and a wave of pronounced pain washed over her face. "Why? Are you embarrassed by me?"

"What?" The question caught him off guard. It was so unexpectedly ridiculous that it was baffling.

"Are. You. Embarrassed. By. Me?" she repeated in a strangled voice, slowly emphasizing each word.

He didn't know how to answer.

"Is that why you didn't tell me who you are? Why you wanted me alone on the boat? So no one would discover you were hooking up with someone like me? Some random American girl. Am I not good enough for you, Mr. Celebrity Formula 1 Driver?"

"What?" he repeated, dumbfounded. Good Lord, this was one argument he'd never anticipated. "No, no! What are you talking about? Why would I be embarrassed by you? Far from it! I didn't…don't want you to be the focus of attention. To be surrounded by all this. To have to deal with the intrusiveness. Wherever I go, people want a piece of me. They follow me. I just wanted some space for us to get to know each other without complications. Privately. Away from this circus. To make it easier on you."

"Oh, get over yourself," Olivia snapped. "You lied to me, *lied*, and now you are suggesting that you only lied to protect me. Stop it. That is some total narcissistic crap right there. And believe me, I know narcissism when I see it. All that flattery, all those cheesy compliments and pickup lines. All lies, right?"

"No, *no*! Don't you understand?!" Niko begged, trying to modulate his voice. "People will record this…our conversation. Every word. You don't get it. You don't want that to happen. Trust me. By tomorrow, we will be all over social media!"

"So what?" Olivia retorted loudly, throwing her arms in the air as an invitation to all onlookers. "What do I care what people record and post on social media? I'm not ashamed of what I'm doing! Are you?"

That did it. The agony of every piece of mortifying content Athena had ever posted with the sole intent to hurt him rose like bile in his throat. Never again.

"I will not do this," Nikos hissed at Olivia. "Not here, not now. I will not."

"Well, that's too bad," Olivia countered. "It's

now or never, buddy. Because after this moment, I never want to see you again. Ever."

Her words were a visceral blow.

"Nikolaes!" Aleko warned.

"Now!" Bryson demanded.

"Olivia!" the wedding coordinator pleaded.

Olivia whirled on her heel before Nikos could reply.

Five hours, one wedding reception, and at least two entire bottles of champagne later, Olivia still hadn't reconciled Nikos's betrayal or recovered from the ugly argument. The whole situation made no sense. Why had he lied about being a baker in the first place? That was just strange. A simple *I don't work at the hotel* would have sufficed. And then, when they spent the day together chasing down pastries, why hadn't he come clean at some appropriate moment? And why had he perpetuated his lie when they were together all day on the boat? In addition to getting to know one another quite intimately, they had talked about everything under the sun. She asked about his tattoos. That would have been a perfect opportunity to confess his real identity.

Not only had he been dishonest, but he'd also gone all in with the deception, made the big splashy gesture, just like her father. Where had the cookies come from? The suspiciously well-produced video of him baking cookies? What was that all about? Was he just a pathological liar?

Or was it a celebrity thing? He'd taken serious

pains to keep her in the dark and hidden from his adoring public. Was it a way to keep his female fan base engaged, encourage them to fantasize that they, too, might have a chance with him? Lies to flatter other women? That, too, was straight out of her father's playbook.

Olivia had no clue.

Worst of all, she couldn't talk to Maggie about it. The bride had other important things on her mind, namely enjoying her wedding reception. Olivia kept a brittle smile pasted on her face. She wasn't going to ruin the most important day of her best friend's life with relationship drama.

So, Olivia drank champagne and ate appetizers. She drank champagne and chatted up her dinner-table companions. She drank champagne and ate cake, purposefully avoiding the cookie table. She drank champagne and hit the dance floor. But when one of the Euro bros got a little too handsy and tried to kiss her while they were dancing, Olivia broke. Summoning her last shred of dignity, she retreated from the ballroom.

Maggie found her fifteen minutes later, in the restroom, splashing cold water onto her face. "You're going to ruin your makeup, Liv."

"I think I'm beyond caring about that, Mags."

Maggie enfolded Olivia in a consoling hug and then handed Olivia a Peanut Butter Blossom cookie. "Are you going to tell me about it or spend the rest of the night pretending everything is fine?"

That did it. The emotions Olivia had repressed

all evening poured forth in a wave of big, gasping, ugly sobs. Maggie made shushing noises and rubbed her back.

"Oh my God, I'm getting mascara on your dress. I'm so sorry. I'm ruining your reception."

"Olivia Keller." Maggie held her at arm's length. "How long have we known each other? And for that matter, how many middle and high school dances did we spend in the bathroom crying over some boy? Why should my wedding be any different?"

Olivia snuffled and broke off the Hershey Kiss. She ate it, then took a bite of cookie. "But I shouldn't do this to you during your wedding reception. I'm so sorry. I did not want to be a distraction. I just wanted you to have your cookies and have the perfect wedding."

Olivia shoved the rest of the cookie into her mouth to keep from crying again. She hoped to keep the cookie and the champagne down. She'd had a lot of champagne.

"Olivia, it might be my wedding, but you are my best friend. You tripped the boy who made fun of my braces at the ice rink. You held my hair when I threw up at that awful fraternity formal. You told off the guy on the cruise who wouldn't take no for an answer. Do you think I'm going to leave you to deal with this all by yourself?"

"I don't even know what this is, what just happened. I don't understand any of it," Olivia wailed.

"Oh, Liv. Only you could accidentally hook up

with the most famous driver in Europe and not know it."

Olivia moaned in embarrassment.

Maggie shook her head in awed disbelief. "Your fight with Nikos gave the wedding guests way more entertainment than they expected. Uncle Klaus is really impressed, by the way. He's a big Segno Rosso fan."

"Then tell Uncle Klaus to hook up with Nikos," Olivia grumbled. "Mags, I feel so stupid. How could I be so stupid? You won't believe it, but for a hot moment, I thought Nikos was for real. After all these years of assuming every guy was as big a liar as my dad, for once, I thought maybe I'd been wrong. Maybe a trustworthy man wasn't some mythical creature and I'd found a unicorn in Monte Carlo. Maggie, I felt it. I thought he was my Meant-to-Be, my M2B."

Maggie smiled fondly at the shorthand code they'd written all over their notebooks when they were twelve years old and agonizing over celebrity crushes.

"Does Harry Styles know you've thrown him over for a Greek F1 driver?" Maggie asked.

Olivia snorted.

"But Olivia, the real question is what are you going to do about Nikos?"

Olivia had no idea.

FRIDAY MORNING

IT WAS REMARKABLE the difference twenty-four hours could make. And not for the better.

Yesterday she'd leapt from the bed and danced around the room, basking in the Monaco sunlight. She'd indulged in incredibly passionate lovemaking with a delicious man.

Now the sky was gray, and rain dulled the city below. Her hotel sheets were stale and sweaty, the goddess-like bronze gown crumpled in a ball on the floor, an unfortunate casualty. She'd worn the dress with Nikos in mind. He was still infuriatingly sexy—but not who he claimed to be. Why were guys such rats? Liars, liars, liars, every last one of them.

She turned on the TV. The weather forecast showed increasing rain and thunderstorms. That squashed her plan to spend this final day in Monaco basking on the beach. Then again, she left her bikini bottoms on the boat. She didn't even want to think about why she took them off. So much for meeting the perfect guy. So much for sunbathing on the Mediterranean shore. The whole trip had gone from debacle to devastation.

Olivia dragged herself to the bathroom, thinking that at this point, like a vampire, she couldn't withstand direct sunlight anyhow.

A shower and a few aspirin marginally improved her physical state. She bundled herself in the snuggly comfort of the hotel robe and contemplated whether her stomach could withstand food. Did she have the energy to get dressed and leave the room, or should she shamelessly splurge and order room service?

She decided the situation warranted a splurge.

However, before she could place the overpriced order, there was a knock at the door. Olivia blessed her best friend as the breakfast trolley was wheeled in.

Who but Mags would even think about anyone else's needs the morning after her own wedding? Who but someone who truly loved Olivia would recognize that breakfast pastries and strong coffee were potent antidotes to hangovers and emotional chaos? Eating away her sorrow was a solid strategy.

As she eyed the pastry selection, another employee entered, bearing a gigantic bouquet. Olivia's gut lurched, which she told herself was entirely caused by her hangover.

There was a card on the flowers.

Maggie wouldn't send flowers. Olivia opened the card with shaky fingers.

I'm sorry. About everything. Please. Will you let me explain?

Grandma wisdom: always eat breakfast.

—Nikos

Damn the man and his *pain au chocolat*. Damn his grandma, too.

Olivia flopped back onto the bed with the pastry and licked her fingers. She suspected she had chocolate smeared across her face. She didn't care.

Fine. She could eat the pastries he provided, but beyond that…what next? What did she want? What did he want?

But first, who the hell was he?

Olivia picked up her phone and googled his name.

It was a mistake. Her mouth went dry, and her gut roiled.

Dear God, nine zillion hits popped up.

He was the subject of a lengthy Wikipedia page.

There were countless images of him spraying champagne on podiums. Blurring around corners in a low-slung red car. Passing under a checkered flag, fist in the air. Close-up shots of his unmistakable azure eyes staring intensely through the narrow slit of a helmet before the start of a race.

She opened Instagram. Oddly, he had no account of his own, but then again, he didn't need one. His name was tagged in pictures, posts, fan accounts, Segno Rosso accounts, F1 accounts, motorsports updates, and product ads. TikTok was even worse.

As he had warned, snippets of their argument

were posted on fan accounts, with horrid comments directed at the unknown girl who dared provoke their favorite crush. Olivia hoped another driver would quickly do something outrageous and supersede her drama with Nikos before it went completely viral.

Even so, she reminded herself that he was the one who would bear the brunt. She was headed back to New York, where literally no one cared about Nikos Leonikaros or any other celebrity.

But until then… Olivia felt nauseous. How incredibly oblivious had she been?

Meanwhile, Nikos must've been laughing his ass off. He couldn't have felt anything for her. Right? The flowers and breakfast were a meaningless grand gesture to assuage his guilt. She'd watched her mother fall for those kinds of gestures, which were inevitably followed by more lies. It was an ugly game. Instead of her dad, now Nikos was playing. Their whole connection must have been a game to see how long he could string along a clueless American girl before she uncovered his true identity.

Could he speed her all over Monaco on his bike? Yes. Could he tempt her to join him on a private yacht for the day? Yes. Could he have sex with her repeatedly? Yes, yes, yes. Damn it, yes. And she'd wanted it. She'd asked for it. Thrown herself at him.

It was mortifying. No wonder he was embarrassed by her.

So much for her New York City street smarts; she had been a total sucker. Totally played.

And at least now she knew how he'd gotten to be so good in bed—plenty of practice. Online there were pictures of him two steps behind every It Girl in Europe. Dodging paparazzi. Attending galas and awards shows. And in each image, he looked achingly, hauntingly, painfully luscious. He rarely posed, but in every candid photo, he was beyond sexy in well-tailored designer clothes and expensive sunglasses, his sun-kissed hair sliding over his face. Like a Greek god.

Should she be grateful that she, a mere mortal, had been touched by a god? Okay, more than a touch. She'd been seduced and seared.

She tried to remember her mythology. Didn't Zeus conceal his identity when seducing mortal women? To her recollection, he did. And sneaky Eros. She should have known something was up when Nikos chose that story.

Damn the Greek gods. All of them.

To hell with it. To hell with Nikos.

But it hurt. It hurt so badly.

No wonder he had hesitated to give her his mobile number.

But she couldn't quite bring herself to block him or delete his texts. Somewhere, in a small, stupid corner of her heart, she held on to a splinter of pathetic hope. She wasn't sure what exactly she hoped for, but damn it, it was there. Hope was an awful thing.

She slammed her phone decisively on the nightstand.

If it was going to rain all day, there was nothing to do but hole up in the hotel room and watch movies. In fact, that was precisely what she needed: watch some cheesy romances, order room service, and have herself a good cathartic cry. And then, tomorrow, she would get on the plane and fly back to New York City. *My night with Nikos Leonikaros* would be a crazy, risqué story she could tell at parties.

She picked up the clicker and tried to navigate the hotel TV. Much to her disappointment, she discovered that European hotel TVs were not designed to provide soothing American rom-com content to the lovelorn. There were French programs, news, and more weather graphics showing incessant rain. And joy of joys, there were sports channels, including multiple ones dedicated to motorsports.

As she frustratedly clicked through her limited options, she became aware of a high-pitched whine emanating from outside. Good grief, was Monte Carlo under attack? It probably was, given her luck and how the trip had gone. The sound grew louder. Olivia pulled back the curtains and watched as a series of race cars screamed past the hotel. Apparently, the Grand Prix festivities had begun despite the gloomy weather.

She peeked out the window again. Was Nikos driving one of the cars she'd just seen? She couldn't help but wonder. She told herself she didn't care if he was.

One of the cars had been red. Wasn't his car red?

Perhaps she could find out. She knew she shouldn't care, but… She clicked back to one of the motorsports channels with English-speaking commentators. Two men wearing rain gear were blathering on in pronouncedly British accents about practice laps, the impact of the weather, and a series of speculations about car configurations, tire strategies, team standings, and racing personalities. It was foreign to Olivia. They might as well have been speaking Greek.

"But our biggest story this Monaco race weekend is Nikos Leonikaros…"

Well, she could relate to that. He had been the big story of her entire trip. She turned up the volume, trying to drown out the noise from the streets below.

She listened as the commentators expounded on the significance of this particular race to Nikos's career. Apparently, he'd won a lot of races. Now he was only one win away from a record-breaking number of Monaco podiums. Olivia swallowed uncomfortably, remembering the Monaco track schematic tattooed on his right hip. She couldn't suppress the memory of how incredible it felt to grip those narrow hips between her legs.

Damn the man.

The coverage cut to commercial. A series of vignettes with a voiceover in French showed Nikos living the glamorous life, flashing a big, blingy watch. Olivia ruefully concluded that the watch she'd seen him wear was, in fact, not a dupe. Her mistake. Who would have thought it? She didn't want to imagine the price tag.

She couldn't stop watching.

When the racing program resumed, the commentators explained they were cutting away from live coverage to present *Nikos Leonikaros: The Enigma*, a thirty-minute feature on the man they described as one of Formula 1's most successful but mysterious drivers.

Olivia snorted and helped herself to another *pain au chocolat*. At least he was consistent. Knowing she wasn't the only one who struggled to figure him out was validating. She opened a leftover bottle of wedding champagne and added it to the fresh orange juice to make herself a mimosa. It was probably a bad idea, but watching a retrospective on Nikos required fortification.

However, as the program progressed, Olivia became confused. And it wasn't the alcohol. Nikos was described as a voracious and brilliant competitor of iron-willed discipline but with an unfathomably aloof personality. Fellow drivers and members of the Segno Rosso racing team offered awed but perplexed depictions of a man who rarely engaged with anyone in the paddock other than when it was time to race. Media clips depicted awkward press conferences, his reticence leaving seasoned interviewers fumbling to fill the gaps in his monosyllabic responses. Even his nickname, "The Enigma," alluded to the mystique surrounding the son of a notoriously reclusive family—a family of eye-popping, staggering wealth. In fact, his net worth meant that he didn't have to trade on his image for additional income. He was said to loathe the social media promotions the team and its sponsors required.

Try as she might, Olivia struggled to align the overall portrayal with the warm, affectionate, thoughtful, down-to-earth person she'd spent two days with. She continued watching, trying to understand, trying to connect the dots. And trying to remember how angry she was at him for lying. It was hard to sustain animosity toward a man who had tempted her to think foolish happily-ever-after thoughts. And baked her cookies. And sent her room service. And never once acted like he had enough money to buy the Taj Mahal three times over.

Damn. She fought to keep the edge on her anger, but it was wavering. Had she misread him? Could there be a legitimate explanation for the lie? Could a lie ever be justified? Experience said no. Every time her dad had cajoled her mother into letting a falsehood slide, a part of Olivia's trusting young heart had died. Their family dynamic had been toxic. But what about Nikos's idyllic descriptions of his family life?

As part of the documentary, historic footage of an impossibly young Nikos zipping around a track as a kart racer included another familiar face. The protective thug who had tried to keep Olivia from confronting Nikos was omnipresent. Who was that guy? What was his role? He'd been with Nikos for a long time. Considering Nikos's upbringing, Olivia wondered if perhaps Nikos had been raised with the idea that a lie was sometimes acceptable or necessary. Maybe he'd known situations in which a lie was warranted? A kindness, even?

As the program concluded, Olivia mixed herself another mimosa. She had a lot to think about.

Thunder sounded overhead, and the chatty Brits returned to the screen, announcing that practice had been suspended because of the weather and would hopefully resume in a few hours.

On cue, there was a knock on her hotel room door.

Nikos stood, dripping wet, in the hotel corridor. But it wasn't the rain that caused him to break into a cold sweat. Yesterday he'd resolved to focus on the upcoming race and relegate Olivia Keller to an appealing possibility for when the season concluded.

That seemingly reasonable decision had lasted until their confrontation. Finding himself on the receiving end of Olivia's fury, he acknowledged he'd been dishonest; he couldn't deny it. But being called out in public, along with her flippant disregard for privacy, had put him absolutely over the edge. It touched raw wounds he thought had healed.

Now, for better or worse, at least everything was out in the open. No more secrets.

Did the truth matter? They would both soon depart Monte Carlo, and the chance conditions that brought them together would no longer exist. In another twenty-four hours, she'd be on a plane to New York, and shortly thereafter, he'd fly to Spain.

He would likely never see Olivia Keller again, so there was little point in making amends and no reason to answer the painful questions she must be asking.

Even so, something in him couldn't allow her to leave, believing he'd been callous or that he'd been embarrassed by her company. Far from it. For a brief, tantalizing moment, he'd actually imagined building a life with her, beyond his career in racing. That shocking realization was easier to admit now that he knew it was impossible.

He owed her an explanation beyond apologies or flowers.

When he knocked, there was a long pause. He knew she was in the room. Would she ignore him? If so, that would be the end of it.

Thankfully, the door opened.

"Was any of it true?"

He admired her tactics. He, too, preferred to take an aggressive approach, assuming control directly from the start.

"I never meant to lie to you. The joke about being a baker was directed at Bryson, my media manager. Then it got awkward because we were spending time together. I tried to stick as close to the truth as possible but didn't know how to tell you. I wanted us to have a chance to get to know each other without the complications and craziness of my life."

She looked like she might slam the door in his face. "That's nonsense, and you know it. All that flattery. Why?"

"I meant every compliment I gave you. Those cheesy lines? They were honest. Every one of them."

He heard the elevator ding. He'd left Bryson and Aleko at the ends of the hall to ward off any fans. He didn't want to give anyone else a chance to overhear this conversation.

"Olivia..."

She glared, offended at his familiarity with her name.

"Can I please come in?"

"What, dodging admirers?"

"Actually, yes. It's why I was using the back entrance when I first met you."

She rolled her eyes but opened the door. He gestured to the chair and she shrugged, so he sat.

Silently, she double-knotted her robe's belt. Remembering how easily the robe had slid from her shoulders the day before and the torrid interlude that followed...he swallowed the lump in his throat.

"First off, please believe I was never embarrassed by you. I think you're incredible. I just wanted to keep everything between us private. That's why

I suggested we go on the boat. Not because I was ashamed of you. Far from it."

"That's your boat, isn't it?"

"Yes."

"But you told me someone else owned it. That's a lie."

"No, I said it had the same owner as…"

"You own the monster yacht, too?! Oh my God, that hadn't even occurred to me."

She dropped down onto the bed, gobsmacked.

It appeared they were going to rehash the past few days, picking apart assumptions, lies, and omissions. His heart sank. This was not how he wanted the conversation to go.

"You told me you wanted to be a baker since you were a kid. That was a lie."

He shut his eyes, ashamed to admit how carefully he'd chosen words to mislead her. "No, I told you I've trained across Europe since I was young. That's true. I started kart racing at age five."

She glared. "Yeah, I saw that on TV this morning. I watched a feature on you. Who knew you were such a big deal? I certainly wouldn't have guessed you warranted a thirty-minute special."

"It was produced by the motorsports network. I honestly had nothing to do with it."

Honestly. He winced at the inadvertent word choice.

"Olivia, I hate that everyone sees my life as content to consume."

She shrugged. "It comes with the territory, doesn't it?"

"It shouldn't. People forget that I'm not some character on TV. I'm a real person. You saw more of the real me than I've shared with just about anyone."

"Do you even know how to make cookies?" she demanded. "I know that video wasn't for me. I saw the full version on the F1 Instagram. Don't tell me that was real."

He shut his eyes and ran his hands through his hair. "I know you won't believe me, but it was for you. Yes, I had to make the video for F1 media. But I despise making social content. Despise it. So, when I was recording, I imagined myself baking cookies for you. You said I appeared to be joyful? It's because I was doing something for you. Sharing something of my family, my grandmother's recipe, with you. You make me feel joy. I feel like myself, not some made-up character, when I'm with you. You have no idea how long since I've felt that."

She paused, considering. He pressed the advantage.

"Yesterday part of the reason I lost my temper was because I knew our argument would be all over social media. I saw fans recording every word. I lost control. I didn't mean to take it out on you. You have every right to be angry. About all of it."

"I mean, okay. Thank you for saying that, but why is social media such a big deal? I get that it sucks, but can't you just ignore it?"

Might as well tell her.

"It's hard to ignore when that's how I found out my previous girlfriend was screwing another driver..."

Her eyes widened. He'd kept the experience bottled up for so long, but now it poured out.

"Athena was my first girlfriend. We started dating as teenagers when I was coming up through the racing ranks. When I made it to F1 and started to be recognized, she took advantage of our relationship to build her own brand, became a celebrity influencer. Then she started a jewelry line...with money I invested. She maxed out my credit cards. All the while, she was cheating on me with...him. Now they have a kid." He shrugged.

"Shit. Okay, that's horrible..." Olivia acknowledged.

Nikos didn't want pity. "Yeah, well, at least I beat him on the track, right? He dropped out of racing, and I won five world championships, partially because I felt I had to prove myself. Prove I wasn't pathetic for letting a woman use me like that. So, screw her. Screw him. Screw them both."

Olivia gave him a long look. He suspected she saw through his posturing.

"It took me a long time to get over it. Maybe I never really did."

"Look, you have every right to be bitter. She sounds awful, but Nikos, I'm not her. The only thing I've posted from this trip is the food I've eaten."

"No, you aren't her. I know that."

"Nikos, the bottom line is that you lied to me. Do you have any idea…the lies I've heard over the years? Every guy I've ever met, including my own father…"

Olivia got up and paced the small room, struggling to continue.

"He promised to always be there for me. He wasn't. He promised to provide for my mom and me financially. He didn't. If I hadn't gotten a scholarship, I wouldn't have been able to afford school. He didn't bother showing up for my graduation. What did it matter to him? What did I matter to him?" She paused to let her words sink in. "You were similarly hurt by your girlfriend cheating and stealing from you, right? Nikos, that's just another way of saying Athena lied. She lied to you…so you know exactly how devastating it is to be lied to. You should understand why I'm so hurt. Why I cannot tolerate lies. Why I never trusted anyone enough to allow them to get close to me. Until you."

She wasn't wrong, but equating his behavior to Athena's gutted him.

"Olivia, I'm not like your father," he insisted. "Nor Athena."

It made him nauseated even to consider he might be anything like his ex.

Olivia pinned him with a look. "Nikos. That's an unconvincing argument, considering you did, in fact, lie to me."

Her words shut him down. There was nothing he

could say. It felt disingenuous to reiterate that this was merely a situation that spiraled out of control and that he hadn't confessed because he couldn't bear to complicate the joy he'd found with her, even in their short time together. Even if that was the truth.

He tried to catch her gaze. "Olivia. I am so sorry…not just for claiming to be a baker, but for everything… You're right. I lied. I shouldn't have. I have no excuse."

Instead of reassuring her, his words appeared to have the opposite effect. He tried again.

"But I want you to know the time I spent with you was real. Going from pastry shop to pastry shop with you on the bike with me…was amazing. And then I wanted to see you again so badly that I didn't want to risk it by telling the truth. So much of my life doesn't feel real anymore, but every time we were together, I tried to show you what I couldn't explain. You make me feel something I've never felt before. And our time on the boat…"

"Don't even mention what we did on the boat!" She looked away, pain evident on her face. "I cannot discuss that right now. And I'm just curious, did you pay someone to make the rest of the cookies? All thirty dozen?"

He paused before answering because he realized she was fighting hard not to cry. Did it mean she cared or that she hated him? Maybe a little of both?

"Yes. I had my staff on the big yacht make them."

She let out a disappointed groan.

"So what if someone else baked them?" he argued. "Yes. I paid someone to make cookies. But you were prepared to pay for them. I helped you. I made the cookies happen, even if I didn't actually bake them. You wanted cookies, I delivered them. For you. Why can't that be good enough?"

She sagged back down onto the bed and covered her face in her hands. "I liked you better when you were a hotel baker."

Now it was Nikos's turn to get up in pace in frustration. "So do I—is that what you want me to say? Because in some ways it's true. Because if I'm a hotel baker, then I know your interest in me isn't about the money and it isn't about racing. It's about me, who I am as a person. I needed to be sure of that. To trust you."

"Trust me? You let me think you had to work two gigs to afford living here. Did you want me to feel bad for you?"

"No! That's not it. I just didn't want you to know I was a driver. But here's the important thing," he insisted, taking a new tack, "I'm done being a driver when the season ends. I told you my contract is ending. That is true. Who knows what my next gig will be? Whatever it is, I can be just Nikos."

"Wrong. Even when you quit racing, this is who you've been since you were a child. Being a driver is as much a part of you as being Greek. You can't erase your history. That was the whole point of the cookie table you helped me with—it's part of my friend's history, even though it's not how she lives now. Don't you see that?"

Her words cut him to the core. He didn't want to admit it, but she had a point. But where did that leave them? Where did it leave him? What next?

Olivia challenged him. "Seriously. How far would you go to erase your history? Your back is covered in racing circuits—would you have the tattoos removed? I doubt it."

"No… I…but…" He switched gears again. "Back to the money…what I spent on the cookies. I meant what I said when I told you money doesn't make any difference."

She scoffed. "Spoken like someone who has never had to worry about money."

"What does it matter?" he snapped. "Your friend…from what you told me about her, I guess she now has a lot of money by your standards. Does it make you think differently about her?"

"She never lied to me about it. That's the point, Nikos. You lied to me. About everything."

They were right back where they had started, at a discouraging impasse. Olivia retook control of the conversation.

"What I want to know is why me?" Olivia asked. She didn't give him a chance to answer. "I'm just a girl who hustles at a job I don't really care about. I live in a three-hundred-square-foot studio apartment, smaller than this hotel room, with a single window looking over a trash dumpster. It isn't glamorous. It isn't Monaco. What could you possibly want with me? Or is this just what you do? Have a thing with a random girl wherever you race?"

"Oh my God, have you heard nothing I said?" he snapped. "It's not like that. I'm not like that. During the season, I focus on my job. Believe me when I tell you that I'm not dating anyone and not looking for quick flings. I've never taken a woman out on my boat for the day, much less overnight. Have I spent time with different women? Yes. Sure. But there's been no one serious. Nothing long-term. I met you and had a glimpse of a possibility between us. I wanted to see where it might go. I thought we had potential. Maybe that's pathetic. I don't know."

He shut his eyes in anguish. "And anyhow, why do you care?"

He felt her grow quiet. He turned toward the window, so as not to see the expression in her eyes. Maybe she didn't care at all.

"Because, because..." she muttered, "I also thought this could be something. I felt like there was something special between us. We could be something."

Why were they having this conversation now, when it was too late?

Yesterday he'd almost convinced himself that as intensely as he had fallen for Olivia, it wasn't the right time; he couldn't get involved with her until the season ended.

So maybe this argument simply confirmed that he couldn't concentrate on a real relationship, especially one that made him feel like he was being ripped open and turned inside out. Perhaps he should cut his losses and move on.

"This has all been really fast," he murmured, testing that theory. But as soon as the words left his mouth, he knew they were cowardly.

"Yeah, well." She threw his words back at him before he could correct himself. "You were the one who said you liked to go fast."

Her sarcastic reference confirmed a harsh reality. There was no way they could make this, whatever it was, work. There just wasn't enough time to make up for his mistakes.

"Olivia, I don't know what to tell you. I came to apologize. I was wrong. I admit it. I told you I wanted to explain and try to make it up to you. I'm not sure you're willing to accept what I'm saying or accept me. I can't argue with you any longer. This is who I am. You see it all now. Take it or leave it."

He'd never escape her hotel room if he stayed any longer. Emotionally, he was wiped out.

"I have to go drive. I had time to stop by because practice was delayed, but now I need to go."

So, would this be the final word? Would his last glimpse of Olivia Keller be of her standing before him in doubt and disappointment?

He was damned either way.

"If..." He was about to say something utterly foolish, but he couldn't stop himself. "If there is any chance of you staying until Sunday, I can send you a VIP pass for Qualifying tomorrow and the race on Sunday. Come. See what my life is like. Then, after the race, we will have time to talk. I can arrange for you to fly home on Monday. Or Tuesday. Or whenever you want. I have a plane. But…but that's all I can do. The rest is up to you. Just let me know what you want to do. Text me. Please."

He stepped closer, silently willing her to accept his offer on the spot. She stood still as a statue, her breathing erratic, hinting at the depth of her emotions. He leaned closer. She didn't flinch, so he kissed her at the edge of her lips and tasted a hint of chocolate.

"Olivia…"

She didn't return his kiss.

With a final sigh of frustration, Nikos slipped out of the hotel room and let the door slam behind him.

SATURDAY MORNING

As HE APPROACHED the circuit for the final practice session, Nikos appreciated that the entire team worked methodically. He'd spent his entire ten-year career with this team. Their preparations provided a framework to function with some normalcy despite his churning emotions. He'd had a rough night. Usually, he got his best sleep during race weekends.

The garage and Segno Rosso headquarters were a world where everyone knew their precise role and function. Eero, Juan-Carlos, and the engineers were analyzing the information displayed on various monitors as they waited for Nikos. They needed to make calculated decisions to form a strategy to successfully perform in the ongoing rain. They could precisely game out possible scenarios and predict outcomes. It was intense, but it was comforting. Familiar. Clear. Unlike his failed romance with Olivia Keller.

The crew was hard at work, readying the car and other necessary equipment. Nikos trusted his car. While in the car, he shared a communication shorthand with his engineer that bordered on telepathic. The mechanics knew how to tweak the car to be maximally responsive to his driving style. And Nikos knew the contours of the Monaco circuit as intimately as the curves of a lover's body. In some ways, the circuit had been his first true love. He had been a seventeen-year-old virgin when he earned his maiden win on this podium. He and Athena became lovers shortly thereafter, and he conquered the race eight more times over the next ten years. One more win and he'd hold the record.

His connection to the circuit was the real long-term relationship. But that was cold comfort in the moment. It was not a relationship that would carry him into the future.

He realized he had precious little time, if any, for a final attempt to talk with Olivia. He looked at his watch. What time was her flight? Usually, transatlantic flights departed in the late afternoon. Was she still at the hotel? Had she left for the airport? Was it too late?

He checked his phone, hoping against hope she'd messaged him to accept his offer of a VIP pass. She hadn't. Should he text her? That felt too pathetic. He wouldn't beg her to stay. At least not yet.

Nikos changed into his kit: the fireproof undergarments, his boots, the balaclava, the racing jumpsuit. Instead of leaving his phone with his street clothes in his private driver's room, he went looking for Bryson.

"Ya." He found the media manager talking to reporters at the edge of the paddock. Camera lenses clicked. Nikos coaxed Bryson far enough away that their conversation wouldn't be overheard. "I need you to do me a favor."

Bryson pulled out his iPad, poised for instructions.

"Get a VIP pass for today and tomorrow. See if you can get some rain gear, too. Here is my private phone. If Olivia texts that she wants to come for Quali or the race tomorrow, then answer and take the stuff to her. Accompany her to the paddock so she isn't by herself."

To Bryson's credit, he took the instructions in stride. "Okay, got it. Olivia texts, go get her. Provide some weather gear. Keep her happy. What if she texts but doesn't plan to attend? What do I tell her? And do you want to know if she isn't coming?"

Nikos winced. "No, no. That would probably be a bad idea. I'll check in with you when I can. Now I've got to get over to engineering. Just use your best judgment, Bryson. I trust you."

"And if I see Aleko?"

Nikos paused. Aleko vocally disapproved of Nikos's interest in Olivia. It wasn't Bryson's job to run errands and carry messages, but he was at least amenable. The old man might take it on himself to give Olivia some off-base advice. Things were messy enough. Nikos didn't need Aleko stirring the pot.

"Nah, don't say anything to him. I don't want to involve Aleko. Thanks, Bryson."

* * *

The screaming whine from cars on the track below provided a headache-inducing soundtrack as Olivia haphazardly stuffed clothing into her suitcase. It was a different approach from the painstakingly organized packing process. There were no fashion decisions to make, no cute outfits to plan. Just dirty laundry and disappointment. It was symbolic of the whole stupid trip.

And she was irritated that she'd lost half of her bikini. With the opportunity to hit a Mediterranean beach, she had justified the expense of buying a nice bathing suit. Now she would have to spend money on a new one if she wanted to do any more beach going this summer. And for what? A poor decision on a boat? She should have kept her bikini bottoms on.

Damn the man.

It was far easier to stay angry at him than to entertain what-ifs. But deep down, those what-ifs still tantalized. If only she had a little more time to maybe, possibly, sort things out.

There was an expected knock on the hotel room door.

"Hi, Mags…"

Olivia did a double take. It wasn't Maggie.

The smooth-talking man who often accompanied Nikos stood in the hallway. Olivia wedged her foot behind the door in case he thought he could barge in.

"Can I help you?" She ensured her tone made it clear that she did not welcome his presence.

"We've not been properly introduced. I'm Bryson Samuelson, Nikos's PR and media manager."

Olivia stood silently, waiting. Why would Nikos send an underling? Let him state his piece and leave.

"I brought you these." Bryson held out a pile of Segno Rosso racing gear.

"And what is this?"

She already had Nikos's sweatshirt, hat, and sunglasses. She didn't need any more mementos. Her gut clenched—did this guy think souvenirs would buy her off? She wondered what the going rate was for discouraging celebrity girlfriend wannabes. If she had no integrity, she could probably recoup the cost of the entire trip.

"VIP passes for today. And rain gear because it's going to be wet. Practice is happening right now—Qualifying will be at four o'clock. The race is at three o'clock tomorrow, but there will be a Drivers' Parade beforehand."

"I won't need any of it because I'm leaving for New York today."

The media manager hesitated. "Maybe just take it, in case you change your mind."

"Did Nikos send you?"

Bryson shifted his weight. "Not exactly."

Olivia raised her eyebrows.

"He told me to have the passes and the gear ready in case you texted that you want to come to the race. He hoped you would contact him, but he's in the middle of practice. I'm supposed to be watching his phone for your message."

The image of Nikos waiting for a text thawed some of the ice around her heart. But not entirely.

"I didn't text him. That should have been a sign."

"No, you didn't." Bryson shook his head. "But I have to go pick up his family. They're coming in for the race. I thought I'd drop this stuff off with you before I left. In case you decided to see what his life is all about."

Bryson shoved the stuff at her. "Look, just think about it. Whatever is happening with you two, it is good for him."

And me? Olivia snorted. *Is it good for me?*

"I'm sure he is acquainted with plenty of women who might be good for him. I looked him up. He apparently doesn't lack for female companionship. I'm sure he'll have plenty of fan girlies to cheer him on."

Bryson sighed. "Don't believe everything you see."

"Or everything I hear from him? He lied to me. He didn't tell me about any of this." She waved her hands vaguely to encompass the enormity of it.

Bryson frowned. "He omitted a lot. Yes. But he found time for you during a race week. That doesn't happen. Ever. And forget about anything you see online or in the media. Look, it's my job to shape how the public perceives Nikos Leonikaros. It's not easy. When someone is as private as he is, it gets interpreted as being mysterious. And people love nothing more than a good mystery. So, the fans become even more fixated on everything he does. If he is seated next to someone at an event, inevitably there's a photograph. Then speculation that they're dating, whether they are or not. Photographers are always present to take pictures—he's eager to be done with that. He loves racing but has achieved almost everything he wants to as a driver. Soon, it will be time to move on, get out of the spotlight. But he's not quite sure how. Or what comes next. And I think you might be the person he needs to help him figure it out."

"Whatever." Olivia shrugged. "I can take the gear and the passes, but don't take it as a sign. Don't tell him I'll be there, unless you want him to be disappointed. I am getting on a plane this afternoon. Maybe I'll check the race results when I get back to New York. I'm sure I can find out anything I need to know."

Bryson persisted. "Yeah, well. Just think about it."

Olivia heard the elevator ding, and thankfully, Maggie appeared in the hallway.

Bryson nodded and excused himself.

"Who was that?" Maggie asked.

"Nikos's PR guy."

"What did he want?"

"For me to forgive Nikos for lying and show up at the race to cheer my favorite driver on to victory.

Rah, rah. Because it would be good for Nikos. Forget about what might be good for me."

Maggie followed Olivia into the room. Olivia flopped face down onto the bed.

"God, Liv, I hate saying goodbye to you like this."

Parting from her best friend was always awful, but it felt a thousand times worse than usual. Olivia wasn't ready to say goodbye or leave the cocoon of the hotel and its plush robes.

Maggie sat down and hugged her. "Admit it—you are a lovesick fool, aren't you?"

"Oh my God, don't be sympathetic. It will just irritate me," Olivia insisted.

She'd maintained a cool attitude with Bryson but wasn't sure she could sustain such nonchalance with her best friend. But she had to try. "And I'm not in love. I've been had by a duplicitous man. And I know all about that, so don't try to tell me otherwise."

"Okay, babe, let's see if I can restate your situation," Maggie paused. "Olivia, I am so sorry you came to Monaco, stayed in one of the most glamorous hotels in Europe, ate *pain au chocolat* twice daily, and enthusiastically slept with a hot F1 driver who's one of the wealthiest people in the world. You scored a ridiculous amount of racing swag and a pair of expensive sunglasses. This trip must've been awful for you. My heart breaks. Oh, and you spent quality time with me, your best friend. That counts for something, right?"

The irreverence made Olivia feel a little better, and she managed half a smile. "Well, since you put it that way..."

Maggie looked at her sympathetically. "So, have you spoken to him? I'm sorry I couldn't fully check on you in person yesterday. I had to spend the day with Stefano's family."

"I understand. And yes, I did talk to Nikos. He showed up at my room unannounced," Olivia admitted.

"And?"

"He tried to explain, tried to apologize. He says he only claimed to be a baker as a joke, but then it got out of control. I didn't question it at the time because I was tired and trying to obtain your cookies..."

"Which he provided," Maggie interrupted.

"Yes, but he lied. It was all a lie. Just like my dad."

"Is he really like your dad?" Maggie asked. "Your dad lied to serve his own selfish purposes. From what you've said, Nikos wasn't selfish. Far from it."

"Okay, maybe he's not selfish," Olivia admitted. "But even so, I googled him and blew through all my international cellular data. Total mistake. You are right—he's famous. Like *famous* famous. I watched a thirty-minute documentary on him yesterday. And Mags, the celebrities he's dated? All over Instagram. Oh my God. It's completely intimidating."

Olivia collapsed back onto the bed. It was all so ridiculous. Maggie snuggled up beside her, and they stared at the ceiling together.

Olivia sighed. "Okay, true confessions. I'm head over heels for this guy. I'm desperately hurt and confused and don't know what to do. My head and life experience say to forget him. He lied. And a celebrity wouldn't want anything authentic with someone like me anyhow. It would all be lies. But… my heart says otherwise. I just can't help it. But I am getting on an airplane in—" she paused to check the time "—five hours."

"First of all, you don't give yourself enough credit, Liv. You never do. Why wouldn't he be attracted to you and want to be with you? You're wonderful. And seriously, social media? You can't trust what you see there. You know that."

"Okay," Olivia admitted. "Let's say you are correct. There is more to him than what shows up on TikTok. Great. Agreed. But Mags, it doesn't change the fact that he lives this crazy life that is so far from anything I could ever imagine. How can I possibly believe I might have a place in his world?"

Maggie was silent for a long moment, her head on Olivia's shoulder. She took a deep breath and let it out in a long sigh. "Are you forgetting where we grew up? We thought being a high school cheerleader was the pinnacle of existence. Back then, Switzerland was not on my radar. But we did our semester abroad. I met Stefano. Do you remember?"

Olivia nodded. "At the bar in Spain. Tapas, Rioja, and destiny."

"Right," Maggie continued. "And before the sun came up the next morning, I knew he was the guy I wanted. Meant-to-Be. M2B, baby."

Olivia sighed. "I hear you, but I'm not sure I can be like you. Becoming a part of Nikos's life might be too big a hurdle. It's all part of the lie. Did you see the monster yacht the other night? That's his. I wouldn't know how to live like that..."

"Oh, come on." Maggie snorted. "I mean, Nikos must have a pretty nice lifestyle, to say the least. Most people would find a way to adapt. You moved to New York City and learned to live completely differently from how you grew up. What's to say you can't make a change again? The question isn't about money, although money makes a lot of nice things possible. The question is whether you want to go for it with him. Is he worth it? But don't refuse because you are insecure or your pride is hurt or you're still suffering from your dad's failings."

Olivia swallowed down that accusation without comment. She suspected it might be entirely too accurate.

She glanced at the time. "Oh my God, Maggie, I've got to call for the car right now or I'm going to miss my flight."

As Olivia picked up the hotel phone to arrange transportation, her cell phone buzzed from the credenza where she'd dropped it. She and Maggie stared at the device. Was it Nikos? Once again, she felt that pathetic glimmer of hope. She hung up the hotel phone.

She looked at the text message. And moaned. "I can't believe this is happening. I don't need to call for a car because my flight has been canceled. Forecasted thunderstorms. Not delayed, canceled."

Maggie gaped, wide-eyed. "You are either exceedingly unlucky…or maybe it's a sign?" she suggested.

Olivia frowned. "A sign of what? A sign that I hate French transportation? A sign that, other than your wedding, this whole trip has been a debacle? And don't try to convince me otherwise."

Maggie's lips twitched. "If you say so. But now you have a flight to rebook, and I have an appointment with Céline to review the wedding account. Tonight we're meeting Uncle Klaus and Aunt Kiki for dinner at Alain Ducasse. Come to dinner. I'll add you to the reservation. Good food always helps."

Olivia moaned. She'd heard that before.

"Okay, thank you. I guess I'm staying in Monte Carlo whether I want to or not."

"So it's a good thing I booked some of the rooms through race day. I'll let Céline know you're staying. Love you! See you at dinner! Think about what I said."

Apparently, Olivia would have at least one more day to consider the situation with Nikos. She wasn't sure if it was a curse or a gift.

SATURDAY AFTERNOON—QUALIFYING

THAT MORNING'S FINAL practice had been wet but largely uneventful. Nikos kept his focus and took the circuit confidently. He secured one of the fastest practice lap times, which was what he needed. Now he just had to push a little harder in Qualifying to ensure he kept the lead. Quali laps were critical. They determined pole. In the precise, tight corners of the Monaco circuit, if he started the grid in first position, it would be unlikely that anyone could prevent him from staying out front and winning the race.

"We need to get you out before the weather worsens," Eero confirmed. "I wish we had more time, but we don't."

The forecast called for the rain to increase, with a high probability of a thunderstorm. Nikos usually wasn't part of the scrum of drivers who took to the track during the congested first minutes of Q1. He didn't need to be. But today strategy called for him to accomplish a fast lap as early as possible.

When it was time, shielded by a crew member

holding an umbrella, Nikos positioned himself at the car. He plugged in his earphones and put on his neck collar support, helmet, and gloves. A mechanic removed the car cover and extracted the steering wheel from the car. Nikos lowered himself into the tight cockpit. His supportive safety devices and harness were connected. The steering wheel was locked back into the car.

"Radio check—confirm you can hear me."

He confirmed. It was time.

With a sharp bark and a jolt, the engine snapped on. Idling, the car whined, metallic and shrill. The chassis trembled, vibrating through every molecule in his body. During these moments, his breathing and heart rate pulsated with the engine, and he felt almost one with the car. All external thoughts and consciousness gave way to utter focus. The anticipation, this adrenaline, this was why he raced. Waiting. Waiting.

"Q1 Started—Pit Exit Light Green."

The tire blankets were whipped away; the jacks dropped the car. With a signal from his team, he was off.

Minutes later, the lap concluded, and he was back in the pit lane. It was a decent lap. Good by anyone else's standards. But not his best. Would it be enough? He hated going out early. Better to wait and know what he was up against.

The clock counted down to zero, and the checkered flag waved, signaling the end of Q1. The slowest drivers would be eliminated and start from the back of the grid on race day. Fortunately, Nikos's lap sufficed. Both he and his teammate advanced to Q2. So far, so good.

The rain had picked up, although the track now held more rubber, which made it easier for the tires to grip. Over the radio, the team debated tire choice for the next round, and Nikos's risky opinion prevailed. He was vindicated when he put down the day's fastest Quali lap. Juan-Carlos did his part with a quick enough time to also advance to Q3. Everything was going according to plan for the Segno Rosso team. At least something was going right in his life.

It was in Q3 that disaster struck.

Olivia headed toward her room later that evening, full and sleepy after another exceptional meal. That in and of itself made the extra day in Monte Carlo almost worth it. She told herself that when she returned to her room, however, it was time to rebook the flight. She had to get back to New York. Right?

She meandered into the room. Without bothering to put down her purse or take off her shoes, she fumbled with the clicker to turn on the TV. Might as well check the motorsports channel for updates.

The chatty Brits were back like old friends. It came as no surprise that they were talking about Nikos. Apparently, he was always the big story. She hated to admit it, but that had to get old, always being the focus of such unwavering attention. He had a valid complaint.

"What do we make of Nikos Leonikaros today?" the first commentator asked.

"Woo-hoo, he had a doozy of a day!" his partner replied gleefully. "Quite a scare for Segno Rosso!"

Scare? Her curiosity piqued, Olivia dropped her purse, kicked off her shoes, and anxiously turned up the volume.

"After the crash today, Segno Rosso must be questioning their decision to send Leonikaros out on intermediate tires!"

Crash?! Olivia felt like she'd been punched in the gut. *There was a crash?!* The commentators appeared to be matter-of-factly discussing whatever mishap had occurred. Surely if Nikos were injured, they'd be talking in less gleeful tones. Surely.

"So was it the tires? I think we can attribute this mistake directly to Leonikaros. We've not seen this kind of reckless performance since he got in a bad situation in Barcelona three years ago!"

Okay. Whatever happened to Nikos, it didn't sound life-threatening. Hopefully, it was just a minor incident. Racing drama. Which was, admittedly, his whole life.

But was he okay? Couldn't the commentators talk about that instead of tires?

Olivia felt queasy, desperate for reassurance, and horribly suspecting their argument had impacted Nikos's driving.

"The question is why? This is not the Nikos Leonikaros we've come to expect. He's dominated every Monaco race since his Formula 1 arrival.

He is a ferocious and laser-focused competitor, which makes this kind of hotheaded performance so strange. He doesn't make mistakes. So what went wrong?"

Olivia hated that she might have contributed to the answer, whether the commentators knew it or not. The internet girlies would be sure to cast blame.

"Let's look at the replay..."

Olivia watched Nikos's red car slice through the impossibly tight, winding Monte Carlo streets. Traversing those streets on the back of a motorcycle had been terrifying enough. How could a car manage at high speeds? And in the rain?

"He dominated Q2. Fastest lap of the day! But then, his Q3 lap attempt is like he's an entirely different driver! Look at how he deviates from the best line. He's skimming curbs, brushing too close to barriers. Some courses might forgive, but not Monaco. He is flirting with disaster from the moment he leaves the pit. Watch!"

Olivia held her breath as the second commentator picked up the narrative. She didn't want to watch but couldn't look away.

"Let's see exactly where the problem occurs. Here's Leonikaros through the second-to-last turn. He's coming in at a high speed... We see that he's already too hot..."

"As he makes the turn and enters the blind apex, coming out...here! We've got O'Sullivan and Yakimoto in a kerfuffle! Yokimoto has spun out in the rain, blocking Leonikaros. And here…"

Olivia gasped in horror as Nikos's car plowed into the stalled race car, sandwiching it into the already wrecked third car. Those vehicles seemed to disintegrate on impact, but somehow, Nikos's car remained intact and moved with enough momentum to tilt sideways onto two wheels, teeter, and then ride grotesquely along the length of a side barrier, shedding parts, until it flipped entirely over—on top of Nikos.

Olivia nearly puked.

"Quite a scare, that! Let's look at the replay again and have a listen…"

A static-filled audio recording with subtitles popped up on the screen.

"What the…?" She heard the split-second surprise and a string of Greek curses.

Crashing, crunching, crushing sounds followed. Then silence.

"Nikos—mate, are you okay?" crackled across the line.

There was a heart-stopping pause.

"Yes, yes… I'm okay. Just give me a minute. Mick and Haruto—are they okay?"

Nikos sounded dazed. But alive. Thank God, alive.

"They're fine. Everyone is fine."

"Good. Good. Can someone get me out…?" His voice was shaky, but he was coherent.

Trembling, Olivia watched footage of a bevy of

track workers shifting pieces, righting his cockpit, detaching his steering wheel, and supporting him as he climbed out. Similar groups were helping the other two drivers while race officials waved red flags. Nikos stumbled for a few steps, assisted by a hovering medic. He turned back to reconnect his steering wheel, even though the car was in no shape to go anywhere. Only one tire remained. The wings and rear tail lay in tatters.

"So now, instead of taking the first slot on the grid as expected, Segno Rosso must contend with Leonikaros having no set time from Q3. At least his fast lap in Q2 secured him tenth position on the starting grid. But will he be able to race at all? This is not the victorious, career-defining Monaco race we expected from Nikos Leonikaros!"

The commentary was overwhelming; Olivia snapped off the TV. She couldn't listen to or watch any more of it. She couldn't shake the image of Nikos's car tumbling over and over, crushing him beneath. She couldn't unhear the hideous sounds of impact. How horrific must it have been for him, trapped in what could have been a death box?

Had their argument contributed to his wreck? Had it distracted him? Did it cause him to lose focus?

She might've been upset with him, but if he had been hurt or, worse, killed… Olivia couldn't even admit to that blood-chilling possibility. He was alive. That was all that mattered.

She reconsidered their situation in a different

light. She'd been so stubbornly angry at his deception that she never stopped to consider what it meant to drive a Formula 1 car, the risk he took every time he took to the circuit. Racing changed the whole context of their conversation. She'd been too furious to see it.

Yes, he'd lied. He'd kept an essential part of his life hidden. But admittedly, if she had first known him as an F1 driver, it might have changed her entire perception. Exactly what he wished to avoid.

And…if she was being truly honest, well, she'd lied, too. She wasn't sincere enough with him—or herself—to admit how her past made it almost impossible for her to trust a man. She'd blithely pursued Nikos as a meaningless fling merely because he offered to help her and was incredibly attractive. She had realized her mistake, but it didn't change the fact that when they first met, she never would have considered the possibility of a genuine relationship. Maybe it was time for both of them to face the truth.

Without giving herself time to reconsider, she picked up her phone.

Nikos gingerly rolled over. Of the crashes he'd experienced, the day's unexpected mishap wasn't the worst wreck in terms of how battered he felt, but he was still banged up. After a thorough medical examination, he'd been cleared to race. Of course, that assumed the team could repair the car in time.

Even though they could work miracles, he should not have put his team in this position.

He winced as he eased onto his already problematic shoulder.

The whole situation was entirely his fault. Q1 and Q2 had gone precisely according to plan. There had been time after his successful Q2 lap to get out of the car. But rather than staying close and concentrating on Quali, he had gone to the paddock looking for Bryson. It was a poor decision, but he'd needed to know—had Olivia texted? Was there any possibility of her staying in Monte Carlo a little longer? Attending the race? But Bryson was nowhere to be found, which meant Nikos's phone and any communication from her were also inaccessible.

Aleko had spotted Nikos. The nosy old man had handed him Olivia's bikini bottoms, which she'd left on the boat, and then wheedled it out of Nikos that he was desperate to hear from her. Predictably, Aleko berated him for thinking about anything other than the task at hand, specifically a fast lap in Q3. Even though Aleko was right, Nikos had pushed back. Hard.

The start of Q3 had interrupted their argument. If there was one thing Nikos knew, it was that getting into the car in the heat of emotion was a mistake. But that was exactly what he had done. And paid the price.

Well. He'd have to make it up tomorrow.

P10 put him at a disadvantage, but he'd taken other unlikely podiums.

There would be a million media questions. Rampant speculation on social media.

He had no answer, but everybody would want a sound bite. They didn't care what he thought or said; they merely wanted him to support their narrative.

At least Olivia hadn't wanted a sound bite, an easy answer. Although his final conversation with her had been frustrating, at some level, he was relieved she finally understood him.

But could he convince her to give him a second chance? He didn't deserve it. And she'd already departed. They were an ocean apart. Was it worth the attempt?

He wondered if during the long flight, she felt any regret that they parted on bad terms. Would it be possible to repair their fledgling relationship? There was a Canadian race in a few weeks. How far was Montreal from New York City? Close enough for her to easily attend? Or could he schedule a stopover in New York? Or maybe she could come to Austin in the fall. Or Las Vegas. He'd put Bryson in charge of the logistics. He simply wasn't willing to give up on Olivia Keller yet. Not a chance.

He knew he needed sleep, but a comfortable position remained elusive. Racing while injured and exhausted would be disastrous.

Rest. Rest. He had to rest.

Thirty minutes later, still tormented by thoughts of Olivia, he gave up on sleep and rechecked his phone. He opened her text thread to reread it, hoping to glean some encouragement.

Shockingly, three dots flickered—was she texting him?! Right at this moment?! From the plane?

He jerked upward too quickly, which hurt. He sank back onto his pillow, staring anxiously at the screen.

The dots disappeared…and reappeared. His pulse accelerated every time she restarted but didn't complete the message. *Come on, come on*, he mentally urged. *Send me something. Talk to me.*

Finally, a text came through.

Hey, are you ok? I saw the wreck

He was surprised she'd seen footage and embarrassed that the crash was her introduction to his abilities as a driver, but it pleased him that she cared enough to reach out. That had to be a good sign, right?

I'm ok. A little sore

It looked awful. Terrifying. What happened?

Stupid mistake

Maybe this is dumb, but did our argument have anything to do with it?

Oh Lord, he couldn't let her feel guilty. Not for

one second. There was no one to blame other than himself.

No, no. Not your fault. Really. I was careless

...but I'm so glad to hear from you. Did you land in NYC yet?

Nope. What will you do now?

Was she talking about the race? Or in general?

Try not to dwell on past mistakes. Fly by the seat of my pants. Make it work

Will you race tomorrow?

Probably, but I'm not talking about racing

There was a long pause. The dots flickered, again disappearing and reappearing. Did she not want to get into it by text? Was texting too impersonal? Should he call and try to catch her when her flight landed?

Her reply came through.

I get it

She made no promises, but her simple, compassionate words brought to the surface every experience and emotion from the previous week. His body flooded with the tantalizing and unanticipated joy of meeting her, the profound and intimate connection they'd shared on the boat, the anguished frustration at his lie's impact, and, finally, the wreck's concussive jolt. He'd always kept strong feelings to himself, tightly regulated. Repressed, even. But in the darkness of his hotel room, bruised in body and soul, he couldn't exert his usual iron will. Couldn't regulate his emotions or keep them zipped up. Couldn't contain his desperate yearning for her. Didn't want to.

I wish you were still here. I'm sorry about everything. I want to make it right

He knew he'd have to wait for a response to that declaration. It was probably too honest. He hoped she'd be receptive to his apology someday, but he suspected it was too soon for her to forgive him. But he had to keep trying. It would be challenging. But he liked challenges.

She answered more quickly than expected.

You should get some sleep so you can race tomorrow

Okay. She didn't acknowledge his apology but still expressed concern for him. That was fine. It was enough for the time being. He could work with it.

Ok. You too—try to get some rest...not always easy on a plane

I'm glad you are okay

Olivia?

What?

God, how to condense the breadth of his feelings into believable texts. No more lies.

I don't want things to end between us

...I could never be ashamed of you

...whatever it takes, can we start again?

...don't answer now, just think about it

He didn't want an immediate response because he was too afraid she'd say no. He needed to live in hope at least until after the race.

I'll think about it

...Good night Nikos

Kalinixta, Olivia

Finally, he dropped off to sleep.

SUNDAY—RACE DAY

OLIVIA PAUSED IN the hotel hallway, poised to knock. Did she really want to do this? There were still seats available on the afternoon flight to New York. If she booked and left Monte Carlo immediately, she would still make it to the airport on time. Shc could…

No.

She'd made up her mind to see this thing through. The horror she'd felt watching footage of the wreck and Nikos's sincere late-night texts convinced her that, despite everything, she still cared for him. Deeply. As she'd never cared for any man before. Might even be falling in love with him.

He had been untruthful, yes. But unlike her father, she acknowledged the lie hadn't been at her expense. Far from it. In fact, she couldn't find fault with a single moment they'd spent together up until the confrontation on the patio. And given everything she'd come to understand about him, in a strange way, he had been honest with her about who he really was—just not about his job.

But if she gave him another chance, it would be on her terms.

She rapped sharply.

Aunt Kiki, wearing a plush hotel bathrobe, opened the door to a large suite. She beamed at Olivia. "Hello, my dear! I am so glad you accepted our offer! Come in, come in. Have some breakfast."

Olivia followed Kiki and settled near the breakfast trolley.

"Help yourself! Klaus is still getting dressed."

"Are you sure you don't want to go to the race?" Olivia asked as she served herself some eggs.

"Oh my goodness, no! I've seen enough Grand Prix races to last me for a lifetime."

"I appreciate it," Olivia said. "I have the VIP pass, but I'd feel strange showing up alone. I don't know anyone or anything about racing."

"Klaus will be happy to provide any explanation you need. He will be so tickled to attend the race with a lovely young lady, he'll talk your ear off. And you'll be sitting directly across from the pit lane, so if you take advantage of that VIP pass, it will be easy to find your friend Nikos."

She had a knowing twinkle in her eye. Aunt Kiki might be ambivalent about racing but apparently enjoyed matchmaking.

Uncle Klaus emerged from the bedroom. Olivia's eyes widened. Gone was the urbane Swiss banker. In his place was a superfan.

The older man wore a shirt circa 1980, judging from its style, coupled with a pair of extraordinary leather lederhosen with the Segno Rosso logo and racing motifs embroidered on the suspenders and pockets. He topped off this notable ensemble with a Segno Rosso newsboy cap.

Aunt Kiki caught Olivia's eye with the universal expression of a woman questioning her partner's sartorial choices. "Klaus was quite the fan of an Austrian driver who raced in the early seventies," she explained with a wink before turning to her husband. "Klaus, dear, you really must wear a raincoat. It's going to be wet." She held up a blinding neon-yellow slicker.

"But won't that hide my clothes?"

Olivia suspected this might be Kiki's ulterior motive.

"We could trade so you could use my raincoat," Olivia suggested. "It's an official team jacket."

"Well! That's a different story!" Uncle Klaus accepted the coat gleefully. In exchange, Olivia took his yellow slicker. She hadn't known what to wear to a Grand Prix race, so she'd opted for a short linen romper. She wore Nikos's cap, with her hair in two long braids. If she had to sit in the rain, at least it would keep some water out of her eyes. No matter what, she was going to look like a drowned rat before the day was done. Might as well wrap up her time in Monte Carlo as bedraggled as when she began.

She and Uncle Klaus made quite the pair.

At dinner the night before, the older gentleman had asked Olivia how she met his current favorite driver. Aunt Kiki quickly discerned that Olivia's interest in Nikos had nothing to do with racing and diplomatically turned the conversation. But after dinner, Kiki quietly offered to surrender her ticket, should Olivia wish to attend the race. Before Olivia could refuse, Maggie enthusiastically accepted on Olivia's behalf.

Olivia wanted to strangle her.

But as they said their final teary goodbye before the happy couple left for their honeymoon, Maggie whispered into Olivia's ear, "Go to the race. If you don't, you'll always wonder what could have been with Nikos."

Especially after seeing the awful wreck, Olivia knew her best friend was right.

So now Olivia was prepared to go to her first F1 race in unceasing rain, to watch her potential lover try to achieve his lifelong goal, accompanied by a grandfatherly man dressed like a mad elf. To say this was just another one of the trip's unexpected hijinks was the understatement of the decade.

Accessing the grandstand was a hike. As they walked, carried along by the crowd, Uncle Klaus kept up an incessant narration of circuit features and turns, histories, and suggested strategies. Olivia's head swam.

Since her arrival, the streets of Monte Carlo had been overrun with racing fans, the hype, the energy, the events, and the crowds increasing daily. Now the excitement had reached a fevered pitch. Every bunting-decorated balcony on every circuit-lining building groaned with people and free-flowing celebration. For the truly well-heeled fan, the harbor contained a flotilla of party yachts.

In the human wave that swarmed toward the circuit, tribal alliances to various teams were evident by each person's apparel. In addition to colorful T-shirts, Olivia witnessed painted faces, signs, and gigantic hats molded in the shape of race cars.

It was bonkers. She saw Nikos's image everywhere—on banners, posters, T-shirts, signs, and video monitors. One devoted woman wore a bikini top with his face on each breast. No wonder he fled to the sanctuary of the sea. Olivia remembered the look of sheer panic when they'd argued in public. Given the level of public fixation she now witnessed, his insistence on privacy was justified. His attitude made perfect sense.

When they finally reached their top-row seats, Uncle Klaus handed Olivia binoculars and pointed. "There you go! Take a look! I like being up high so we can see pit lane. You can see the Segno Rosso garages from here…"

"Is Nikos there now?"

Could she see him? Might he somehow spot her in the crowd? It wasn't very likely. She was one of roughly one zillion spectators.

"Right now, he will be at team headquarters, warming up, meeting with his engineers, preparing…"

"Okay. Is this where the race starts?"

"The starting grid is here, yes. You'll be able to

see the beginning and end of the race. You'll love the podium ceremony…a member of the Monaco royal family presents the trophy!"

It was impossible not to get caught up in the excitement.

However, there was a maddening amount of time to kill before the Drivers' Parade. Olivia thought she might lose all sanity, anticipating the opportunity to witness Niko in his natural habitat.

"Tell me more about driving for Segno Rosso," she prompted Uncle Klaus. The man could talk. He would be an informative diversion. "Why are you a fan?"

"Well," the old man began, "your friend Nikos has incredible intuition. He makes his moves quickly—one minute, a competitor has the lead, the next moment, they are in his rearview mirror. In the blink of an eye!"

Incredible intuition. She'd experienced that.

"Is he truly a great driver compared to all the others?"

It was what the commentators on TV had implied. She never would have guessed it from his humble behavior.

"Yes, absolutely…" Uncle Klaus confirmed. "But that's just one reason I like him. My company is involved with asset management for the Segno Rosso Foundation. Without betraying confidentiality, Nikos Leonikaros does a lot of charitable work in the cities where he races. But at his insistence, there is no publicity around his initiatives."

"He didn't mention that."

Nor had these philanthropic initiatives appeared in any online media. Olivia had no idea how he had hidden something so significant, but she was beginning to understand why.

"His family is equally generous with their wealth," Klaus continued. "Did he tell you anything about them?"

Olivia shook her head. "Just that they live on a tiny private island. I assumed it was rustic, but now I'm guessing that's not the case."

Uncle Klaus had a good laugh.

"Quite the opposite!" He chuckled. "The Leonikaros family has spent immense amounts of money preserving the cultural heritage of Greece. Restoring architecture and artwork. Purchasing antiquities from private collections and donating them to the national museums. Incredible work. But all of it is done utterly behind the scenes. You'll never find the Leonikaros name on the wing of a building."

Damn. It was exactly what Olivia would do if she had that kind of money.

"They are an incredibly private family. No one visits their island unless by special invitation."

Nikos had mentioned joining his family for Easter dinner. Did he see her as someone special? Each new bit of information about Nikos sent her reeling, rethinking every conversation.

He had lied. True. But the picture of him that emerged was more complex. Based on everything she'd learned, Nikos was an incredibly private person from an equally private family. Yet he had decided to share some of himself with her. He wasn't ashamed of her after all.

But she had to keep Klaus talking. Otherwise she'd go out of her mind waiting for the race to start.

"Tell me how you and Kiki met..."

While Klaus waxed nostalgic on clandestine rendezvous at a Swiss boarding school, Olivia recalled her own grandparents. They met at a bar the night before her grandfather shipped out to Vietnam. They'd shared a few too many beers and a hot make-out session in the parking lot. Olivia suspected that it had gone beyond a few kisses. Three years' worth of letters and fifty-three years of marriage followed. Was that kind of love story possible? By focusing entirely on her parents' failed marriage, was she selling herself short, denying a beautiful possibility for her and Nikos? Maybe her parents hadn't managed an epic love story, but her grandparents had.

Abruptly, she realized she had a decision to make. What was the point of attending this race if Nikos didn't know she was still in Monaco? Should she text him? Would he look at his phone this close to race time? Would a text distract him? She couldn't live with herself if she contributed to another crash.

Nikos groaned as his trainer worked his recalcitrant shoulder. It felt like the woman was trying to detach his arm from its socket. He was still stiff from the wreck and would pay for it during the race. He took another long sip of water and fought to concentrate on the music pulsing in his AirPods, trying to lose himself in a laser-focused pre-race mindset.

All things considered, his headspace was good. That morning he'd been so keyed up, he was afraid he might puke. That hadn't happened since he was a nervous rookie. He couldn't risk dehydration. But now his agitation had coalesced into a good energy, an excited tension he hadn't felt in a long time. Starting from P10, this race would pose a significant challenge. He thrived on challenges.

When the punishing massage was done, it was time to make his way through the drizzle to the flatbed float used for the Drivers' Parade. He was thankful that all he had to do was stand with the others like a herd of cattle on a truck. Assuming he could lift his arm above his head, he'd wave. He hated the media circus, but the thousands of fans braving the crappy weather deserved acknowledgment. Hopefully, he'd put on a real show during the race and give the Segno Rosso faithful a treat. But until then… Nikos flipped up the hood of his sweatshirt, trying to remain incognito before he got onto the float.

Once it began, the parade's speed—or lack thereof—was torturous. As the float passed the last grandstand, Nikos gratefully lowered his arm and took one final glance at the appreciative crowd. And then, not quite trusting his eyes, he whipped around and leaned over the safety rail to see more clearly. His view was blocked, so he had to step and squeeze past the other drivers to get to the back of the truck. He squinted at the sea of faces receding into the distance…

He was seeing ghosts. How crazy was it that he imagined seeing Olivia's face in the crowd? He shook his head, annoyed at himself. He was being sloppy. How could he race when every unguarded thought strayed in her direction?

After donning his layers of racing gear, he had a few spare moments in his private room before going down to the garage. He debated for a second, then picked up his phone. By sending her message, maybe he could exorcise his thoughts at least until the race was over.

Race starts soon. Wish me luck. Wish you were here

What time was it in New York? For someone who traveled the globe as much as he did, one would think he could keep time zones straight. He guessed Olivia was at least six hours behind. So, it was still early morning in the US. She probably wasn't awake yet, especially after a long day of travel. He imagined her sleeping in bed in her tiny apartment and, hopefully, dreaming of their time together. She'd see his text first thing when she awoke.

Look across pit lane

Shocked to receive a response, he nearly dropped the phone. It took him a long moment to process the message's implications. And then he thought his heart might stop. Completely cease beating.

Still, just to make sure he understood correctly…

Why? What will I see across pit lane?

A very wet American girl wearing a Segno Rosso hat

ARE YOU HERE????

His entire life balanced on her answer.

I am. Couldn't leave without seeing you again

He sprinted down the stairs and wove through the garage, navigating tools, tires, the car, and the crew.

"Hey, Nikos…" Someone started a question.

"Not now…"

He grabbed an open umbrella from one of the crew and burst out onto pit lane. All nonessential visitors had been cleared from the area in anticipation of the race's start. Nikos had an unobstructed view of the grandstand, but it contained a multitude of people.

He fumbled, trying to hold the stupid umbrella and text simultaneously.

Where are you?

Top row. Grandstand to your left. Look for neon yellow. Can't miss me

He scanned the scene wildly… *There!* It had to be her, top row, waving her arms in the air. She was standing on her seat; she stood higher than the rest of the crowd.

He dropped the umbrella and raised both arms above his head, forgetting all about the rain and the achy shoulder. Nikos signaled wildly, making no effort to hide the enormous grin on his face.

Seeing this atypical display of emotion from their favorite driver, the crowd roared, assuming it was for their benefit. Lenses clicked, countless phones popped up. But for once, he didn't care. All that mattered was that she was here.

Nikos lost sight of her in a sea of flailing arms. But she was at the race. For him. She hadn't left Monte Carlo. It changed everything.

This was a girl who, even when justifiably hurt and upset, had still decided that he was worth showing up for. No girlfriend had ever shown up for him like this.

I have to go now, but Olivia…

What?

He paused. He had so many emotions, so many big emotions. He had to articulate his feelings. Let them loose. Only then would he be able to concentrate on winning the race. One didn't win races or relationships by hesitating or being cautious. At least Nikos Leonikaros didn't.

I might be falling in love with you

His breath hitched, waiting.

Me, too. It happened fast. You like to go fast

...Good luck on your race

In that moment, Olivia was thankful for the rain. It disguised the tears that spilled over seeing Nikos, whole and unharmed. And she couldn't even begin to process his message. Was love possible? Her heart said yes.

He was sexy as hell, even in the rain. For once, he wasn't wearing sunglasses, and she imagined she could see the azure intensity of his eyes, even from so far away. As he waved his arms, the top half of his unzipped jumpsuit hung low, accentuating those narrow hips. He was so beautiful; he drew everyone's attention. But today it seemed he didn't care who watched. The crowd ate him up, but Olivia knew his greeting was entirely for her and her alone.

He disappeared back into the Segno Rosso garage. God, how soon could she see him, talk to him, touch him again? Somehow, they had to make things right between them. He was worth it.

The race preparations were moving at molasses speed. Would the event never start?

Finally, the grid cleared.

Uncle Klaus tapped her on the arm and pointed. "The cars are being released!"

Olivia used the binoculars to track Nikos as he slowly exited the garage and negotiated the narrow pit lane before steering his car to his designated spot on the grid. There were a lot of cars positioned in front of him, which did not bode well for his chances. Olivia wondered if Nikos didn't win, would he want to continue his racing career for another season? Did the prospect of a relationship with her change his perspective? She had no idea. But for today, for his sake, she hoped for a miraculous win.

Once the grid was set, the start was imminent. Olivia began anxiety-sweating in the borrowed rain slicker. What must Nikos be experiencing at this moment? Was he calm? Focused? Determined? Anxious? Or was he thinking about her? She did not want to be a distraction.

"They're calling for a safety car start because of the rain!"

Like baby ducks in a row, cars began to creep

forward on the straightaway, carefully trailing the flashing lights.

At Klaus's suggestion, Olivia listened to the live feed between Nikos and his team.

After four laps parading behind the safety car, an announcement crackled through the airwaves: "Safety car, in this lap."

This was the signal they'd all been waiting for. When the safety car peeled off, the shrill pitch of twenty engines ratcheted. The tidy configuration of cars instantly scrambled. The race was on.

Watching the sheer speed of the vehicles and aggressiveness of the drivers was unlike anything she'd ever witnessed before. Olivia couldn't ignore the hypnotic energy that mesmerized her and pulled her in. With one eye on the stretch of pavement in front of her and one eye on a gigantic monitor, she realized that no video footage could do justice. No wonder Nikos considered their motorcycle adventures to be tame.

One had to admire how the drivers pushed their cars and each other, the hairsbreadth control when overtaking at blistering speeds, the exhilaration of watching cars jostle on impossible turns, and the heartbreak when a car spun out of contention.

As the laps progressed, Olivia couldn't visually follow his car as it made its way around and around the entire city circuit. The monitor showed the leader, cutting to video of other drivers when they experienced mishaps. Three drivers ahead of Nikos had already wrecked out of contention. The loudspeaker commentary switched between various languages. Listening to Nikos's somewhat cryptic messages with his engineer on the team audio feed was only marginally better.

"A lot of water for these tires."

"Copy that. Rain is expected to lighten up. Stay out."

Suddenly, the video monitor switched to an interior view of the famous curving Monte Carlo tunnel, with the camera focused on Nikos's car. Olivia's stomach dropped, unsure if this foretold a disastrous outcome.

"Watch!" Uncle Klaus yelped. "He might overtake!"

Sure enough, Nikos crept dangerously alongside another car in the eerie yellow light, the sounds of their engines amplified in the enclosed space. Maybe it was better that Olivia hadn't seen every risky move he made. It was terrifying.

"Now! Send it!" Uncle Klaus cried.

Olivia gripped the old man's arm and held her breath. Exiting the tunnel, Nikos prevailed and darted deep into the exit curve, forcing the other car out. Segno Rosso fans screamed their approval of the daring move.

Five cars remained in front of him. Olivia willed Nikos on, willed him to use every ounce of his considerable talent to seize a victory. Just, please, God, not to wreck while doing it. Her heart couldn't take it.

Lap after lap, the race progressed. The conversation between Nikos and his engineer remained calm. Despite Olivia's anxiety, he apparently took it all in stride. This was the driver the motorsports commentators had described. She was thrilled to see him in action.

Across from the grandstand, drivers took turns boxing in pit lane with incomprehensible speed. They zipped in and out, seemingly without stopping. Suddenly, one car was delayed. The monitor cut to coverage of a crew unexpectedly struggling to remove a stuck front tire. Nikos was approaching the entrance, having been instructed to make his stop.

"Nikos. P5 is delayed in the box. Possibility to overtake."

"Keep me posted. Approaching pit lane entrance."

"P5 is still delayed. Do not box. You are cleared to overtake if you can pick up the pace. Push it. You can overtake, but it's going to be close."

"Copy. Accelerating."

Nikos's car ran parallel to the delayed car as it attempted to exit pit lane before he could catch up. If he could just gain a bit more speed…

Nikos surged ahead, narrowly cutting in front of the other car as it reentered the course. The crowd roared. Nikos had gained another position.

Four cars were between him and a win. Was there enough time remaining in the race? Was the impossible possible? Olivia was all in, pulling for him to succeed.

One of the leaders sustained damage to a front wing and limped through the tunnel, sparks flying. Three more places to grab the win.

"Nikos. Juan-Carlos in P3 is working to overtake Yakimoto in P2, with a two-second gap. You have a five-second gap."

"Copy."

With only seven laps to go, Nikos's teammate pinched the P2 car and then snuck by with a risky move that sent it swerving over a painted crosswalk. The car spun and bounced roughly over a curb, damaging the front wing. White smoke shot out of the back, and the car stalled. Nikos negotiated the immobile car and accelerated out of the turn. Now only his teammate and one other car—driven by his rival, Mancinelli—were ahead.

"If the Segno Rosso cars can hold out, your young man and his teammate will be on the podium!" Uncle Klaus exclaimed. "That would be a strong team finish!"

But would it be enough? Olivia guessed Nikos wouldn't be content to take second or third place. He needed to win. But as much as she wanted a victory, she dreaded a reckless attempt.

"Nikos. Juan-Carlos will drop back for you to overtake. You are at a two-second gap."

"Hold back? No, I don't want him to cede me a position. What is his gap?"

"Three seconds."

"Tell him to go for it. I'll pick up my pace, and we'll see who wins."

"That's an interesting approach," Uncle Klaus worried. "They are as likely to take each other out and not finish the race at all. Teams should work together."

"I don't think Nikos will want to set a record because his teammate allowed him to pass. He'll want to earn it himself."

Could he do it?

Nikos pushed hard, gaining on the two cars in front of him. His teammate moved erratically, slowing both vehicles ahead of Nikos.

"Nikos. A half second back. Push to overtake."

"Copy that. It's time."

The video monitor remained locked on the three cars vying for the lead. The commentators went bananas, crying out in multiple languages as they narrated the action.

And then, as if in slow motion, Olivia's worst fears were realized. The two lead cars slowed into a tight turn. On the twisting exit, while fighting for position, one car clipped the rear tire of the other. The seemingly insignificant contact triggered a split-second chain reaction. Nikos's teammate's car shot into the air, rolled, and came to rest in a million pieces against the barrier. From the driver's angry gestures, he had obviously survived the wreck. Meanwhile, Mancinelli's car was forced to jerk sideways to avoid the debris. Unaware and in hot pursuit, Nikos roared around the blind corner just as his slowed rival smashed against a barrier. Swerving to avoid the stopped car, Nikos spun with almost balletic grace, his car pirouetting past his damaged competitor and coming to rest facing the wrong direction, one back wheel on the raised curb.

Olivia stopped breathing. Was this how Nikos's Monaco dream would die? Would another car come around the turn and slam into him? Dear God, she couldn't witness another crash.

Fortunately, the announcers stated that a virtual safety car had been declared. Flashing yellow lights warned approaching drivers of the wreckage field.

"There's no passing under a yellow flag," Uncle Kraus exclaimed. "He'll be in first position if he can get straightened out!"

In the narrow corner, with barriers, curbs, and detritus from the other cars, Olivia assumed there was no way for Nikos to turn around in time—if even his vehicle was drivable. There was simply no room to maneuver on the narrowest part of the circuit.

Nikos's car jerked in reverse and then forward. It was functional. He desperately attempted to rotate in the right direction.

Back and forth, back and forth. It was worse than watching a new driver learn to parallel park. Just as the remainder of the field bore down on the corner, Nikos's car leapt forward, headed in the right direction. Nikos took command and eased around the next curve. He had established himself in first position.

"He did it!" Olivia screamed, along with every other Segno Rosso fan.

The crowd collectively held its breath as the field drove two more laps under the yellow flag. Then, for the final two laps, the flag was lifted. Nikos shot forward decisively.

No one knew the Monaco circuit like Nikos Leonikaros. With a considerable lead, smoothly, effortlessly, he coaxed his car through every chicane with a lover's touch. He was in a world of his own, the other cars far behind. His final, flawless laps clinched the victory, icing on the cake.

The checkered flag appeared. As Nikos sailed down the final straightaway, Olivia's pulse raced as fast as the speedometer.

When he shot over the finish line, the crowd's roar was so deafening that it drowned out the shrieking engines of the trailing cars. Olivia leapt up and down, ecstatically hugging Uncle Klaus and anyone else in the immediate vicinity. The entire grandstand rocked and swayed with uncontained rapture.

Over the team audio, she could hear Nikos's jubilant "Yes! Yes!" The gigantic image on the video monitor zoomed in on him in the cockpit of his car. He pumped his fist in the air, his visor flipped up to reveal his brilliant eyes.

The sun came out and bathed the scene in gold. It was a fairy tale. A storybook ending. And she was a part of it.

Olivia was crying. She couldn't help it. She heaved gigantic sobs of relief. Uncle Klaus was not as incoherent.

"Your VIP pass!" Uncle Klaus hollered into her ear. "We need to get you down there! Right now! Go! Go!"

He grabbed her by the hand and, with surprising strength and nimbleness, steered them down through the rows of seats toward the grandstand exit. Where crowds blocked the steps, he hauled himself and Olivia up and over the seats. Clearly, life in the Swiss Alps had rendered the old man part mountain goat.

Trying not to stumble as she was tugged along, Olivia watched on the monitor as Nikos concluded his celebratory lap with a spectacular three-hundred-sixty-degree wheel-shredding, smoke-inducing doughnut spin at the end of the straightaway. The crowd, already euphoric, lost all control. She was engulfed in a pulsating human wave. People surged toward the track, determined to share their hero's glory.

On the screen, Nikos cruised into the special *parc fermé* area next to a signboard showing a large number one with his name. He climbed out, replaced the wheel, removed his helmet, and stood jubilant atop his car. Someone in the seats above tossed him a Greek flag. He snatched it out of the air and waved it over his head, triumphant. He was like a Greek god come to life. Olivia could hardly bear it; she was so damn proud of him.

"Come on, come on!" Uncle Klaus urged.

The entire Segno Rosso team mobbed the circuit fence, chanting Nikos's name.

When they reached the security entrance, Olivia yanked her pass from beneath the neckline of her linen romper. Cleared to enter, she was about to shove her way into the crowd…but first, she turned and gave Uncle Klaus a grateful hug.

"Thank you! For everything," she murmured. "Kiki is a lucky lady."

The old man blushed and nudged Olivia forward. "Go get him, girl!"

She turned toward the fence that separated everyone from Nikos. A sea of people stood between her and the barrier. How was she going to get through and avoid being crushed? But she told herself if she could handle a NYC subway platform at rush hour, she could handle a scrum of race fans. Nikos was worth it.

She placed a hand on a random shoulder and, using it for support, jumped up, trying to see over the heads in front of her.

Not surprisingly, Nikos's bodyguard, Aleko, stood at the front fence. He faced the crowd, scanning faces. Would he help?

She jumped again. This time, the old man spotted her.

Like a bull elephant, he began to muscle his way to her. She wriggled and squirmed between bodies, popping up every few steps to make sure their paths would intersect. Finally, the man thrust a meat-hook hand toward her, and she seized it. Her progress through the crowd became much easier with a human plow.

Near the front of the fence, Nikos had thrown his arms wide and, with absolute trust, dropped backward into celebratory hands. Borne aloft by his ecstatic team, they passed him overhead.

"Nikos!" Olivia vainly screamed his name. How could he hear her? How would he discern her voice from all the others? How could she get his attention? Yes, she would definitely see him later, but she wanted to be with him *now*, now in his moment of triumph.

"Nikos!"

Beside her, Aleko dropped down and patted his knee. Understanding the invitation, Olivia placed a hand on the old man's shoulder for balance and stood tall on his thigh. She screamed Nikos's name again. He twisted around at the sound of her voice.

He surveyed the crowd, searching.

Finally, their eyes locked, and to her, everything else—the chaos, the crowd, the noise—fell instantly silent.

Nikos's face split into a gigantic smile; Olivia beamed approvingly back at him.

Laughing, Nikos coached the crowd to surf him in Olivia's direction. When they dropped him next to her, no force in the world could have kept them apart. Jostled by the multitude, their bodies collided hard.

Everyone was so loud that he had to place his mouth to her ear to be heard. She could feel his breath, hot and quick.

"You're here," he gasped. "I can't believe you're

here. God, Olivia, I was afraid I'd never see you again. I'm sorry—I'm sorry for everything. I've been selfish. I've been stupid."

"Stop. Don't apologize," she reassured him, her arms around his neck, pulling him closer so he might hear her reply. "I understand. And I'm sorry, too. I've been afraid. Afraid I wasn't good enough for you. Afraid to trust you, that you would be there for me."

"Please believe me," he insisted. "I'll always be there for you."

"Only if I can be there for you, too. I'm so proud of you. I liked you as a baker, I like you even more as an F1 driver. But it's all about who you are, Nikos, just yourself. That's what matters to me."

He replied with a devouring kiss.

God, the taste of her. He'd been so afraid he'd never kiss her like this again. The force of their encounter knocked his hat from her head—no doubt someone would grab it as a souvenir. Nikos didn't care. He couldn't get close enough; he needed to feel the sensation of her entire body pressed against his. He felt almost feral. Beyond words. Sheer adrenaline-fueled desire.

Cupping his hands just under the fluttery edges of her shorts, on that delectable stretch of bare skin where her ass met the tops of her thighs, he hoisted her up, bearing her weight. She wrapped those gorgeous legs around his hips, locked her ankles, and twisted her fingers through his hair. She consumed his whole being. Could she feel how hard he was for her underneath his racing jumpsuit? He wanted to escape the crowd and have her up against the nearest wall, to be inside of her, to cause her to moan, and to hear the sound of his name in her mouth. Damn, he never wanted to stop kissing her.

Everyone around them roared at their favorite driver, so typically emotionless, now passionately embracing a beautiful woman. A zillion camera lenses clicked. He didn't care. He was vaguely aware of Aleko trying to hold back the crowd. Someone soaked them with a spray of celebratory champagne, which brought Nikos back to some semblance of consciousness and control.

"Champagne and cookies?" He pulled back from the kiss just enough to catch her hazel gaze. He needed to memorize every freckle, every eyelash.

"The perfect combination," she murmured, kissing him again. "So sweet together."

Soon, he would have to join the imminent podium celebration and accept a trophy from the prince of Monaco, as his family watched nearby. He would have to answer a thousand questions in the mandatory post-race press conference. There would be a race debrief. He couldn't escape those obligations, and honestly, after his success, he didn't mind. It was all part of savoring the victory.

But he'd come so close to losing Olivia. Right now, he needed just a few more moments to indulge in her, indulge in the fact that she had chosen to stay in Monte Carlo for him, even though he didn't deserve it. He needed to convey what her trust meant to him, how he suspected she had become as essential to him as the air he breathed. An idea began to form.

He placed her solidly back on the ground. She looked at him expectantly. Fondly. He always wanted to be the focus of that gaze.

"Come on."

He compelled them both through the crush.

"Where are we going?" She laughingly kept pace, clinging tightly. He loved the sensation of her hand in his; he wanted her at his side, grasping his hand, hanging on to him, forever.

"Trust me," he called over his shoulder. Curious race fans let them pass, eager to witness the unexpected spectacle of a joyful Nikos Leonikaros in their midst.

Finally, the unmistakable blue of the harbor yawned ahead.

Olivia paused, guessing his plan when they arrived at the very end of the pavement. The water lapped enticingly below, and people on the nearby yachts whooped encouragingly.

Nikos smiled wickedly at her.

"Oh my God, Nikos, you don't mean to…"

"I do." He turned, catching both her hands in his and explaining, "It's a tradition in Monte Carlo whenever there is something truly worth celebrating…"

"You go ahead and celebrate, then." She smiled.

"This is your victory. I'm proud of you. You won. You got your record."

"I'm not celebrating any racing wins." He leaned closer to whisper in her ear. He felt the quick, warm intake of her breath. He kissed her on her delicious neck. "I'm celebrating that you came back, that you forgave me. I'm celebrating us. What I think we can be together."

He dipped his chin and raised one eyebrow in invitation. "Are you with me?"

She tilted her head but smiled gamely at him. "I am already soaking wet…"

He winked before catapulting himself airborne off the edge, doing a full flip and splashing into the sea. He bobbed to the surface and shook the water out of his hair. Olivia stepped, laughing, to the edge.

Thousands of voices spontaneously chanted in unison, "Jump! Jump! Jump!"

"Are you sure about this?" she asked.

He was. And she needed to know it.

"I love you, Olivia Keller!" he yelled loudly enough for all of Monaco to hear.

She beamed at him.

"You're crazy, but I love you, too, Nikos Leonikaros! So, I guess that means…" She took a running start, covered her face, and leapt, plunging into the water at his side.

The fans on land and the spectators on the yachts screamed their approval.

She came up sputtering. Awkwardly paddling,

legs tangling, gulping sea water, he kissed her again.

The water around Olivia and Nikos churned. They were in full view of countless other people, but no one else could hear him.

"Olivia, I want you. So badly. Please. We can stay on the big yacht tonight and be in Spain tomorrow morning to see the sun come up. And I have the plane. I can fly you back to New York whenever you need to go, but promise me we'll be together again soon. After Spain, I'll be at team headquarters in Italy. I'm going to Montreal soon…and then a bunch of other races. I'll be in the US for Austin and Las Vegas in the fall. I'll get you a schedule. I can fly you to any of them. Whatever you need. Whenever you want. When I have a break, I'll come to New York. And when my contract is up, we can go anywhere you want. Just please say we can be together."

He was babbling, loopy tired from the race.

Olivia paddled closer and shushed him with a gentle finger on his lips. "Nikos. We'll figure it out as we go along. Fly by the seat of our pants. All that matters is that we trust each other and will be together. I promise we will be."

That was all he needed to hear.

Now they just needed to figure out how to get out of the harbor.

EPILOGUE—ONE YEAR LATER

OLIVIA STEPPED OUT of the shower and brushed back her wet hair. She pulled on a thick white robe that Nikos had sent her from one of the hotels he'd stayed in over the past year on the few occasions they'd been apart.

Not surprisingly, she found him relaxing in his usual spot on the comfy sectional sofa on the superyacht's main bedroom balcony overlooking the ocean, watching one of his favorite movies. Their puppy, Eros, lay curled up beside him. Olivia settled down between Nikos's legs and leaned back.

"I'll bet the red car wins," she commented. "Or at least it did the last ten times you watched this movie."

He nipped her earlobe. "Shush. I like seeing all the old-school cars in this movie."

She leaned back, contentedly, and closed her eyes. "What time will we dock in Monte Carlo tomorrow?"

"In time to see the sun come up."

Olivia smiled. "Perfect. That will be spectacular.

While we are there, I want to take Mags and Stefano out from Beaulieu-sur-Mer on the small boat."

"That's fine," Nikos agreed. He interlaced his fingers with hers. "But I also want the two of us to go out alone."

"Oh, absolutely." Olivia grinned, remembering the intimate Mediterranean adventure that started it all. "I like that plan."

She lifted his hand, kissed it, then inspected it closely. "I can't believe you already got a wedding band with my first initial tattooed on your finger. We aren't getting married until October. You've got three more months yet."

"I was in Italy at the tattoo shop to add my Austin podium, so I thought I'd get the ring tattoo while I was there..."

Olivia laughed, but his unwavering commitment warmed her to the core. "You'll be back in Italy before the wedding. You could have waited."

He shrugged. "Yeah, I'll probably go back twice more before October. But I'm not going to change my mind about getting married. Not going to change my mind about the girl. So, I got the tattoo while I was there."

Nikos had accepted a consulting position with Segno Rosso. He regularly visited their Italian headquarters and test track to refine developments on the prototype cars and work with younger drivers. After she'd resigned from her old job, Olivia was free to travel with him and to visit Maggie in

Switzerland to work on a project close to all their hearts.

"I must admit, this tattoo is my favorite..." Olivia turned his hand over to reveal the small *M2B* tattooed on the inside of his wrist. For their first Christmas together, he had given Olivia a gold necklace with the same code in diamonds. "You are the embodiment of my middle school–notebook doodles. I heart Nikos."

Nikos nuzzled his face in her damp hair. "I heart Olivia. I heart how she smells. I heart her wearing a bathrobe."

She couldn't help it. Olivia cracked up. "You weirdo. Most guys would think their fiancée looks hot in a bathing suit..."

"You do."

"...or sexy lingerie."

"Absolutely sexy."

"...or a gorgeous dress."

"Stunning."

"But a bathrobe? I look like the Stay Puft Marshmallow Man's girlfriend."

"Hey, I've kept up my training, so don't call me a marshmallow. And it isn't how you look in a bathrobe, you goof," he explained as his hand slid underneath the garment in question. "It's the ease of access that I appreciate."

"Ah," Olivia murmured. "I begin to understand."

He proceeded to do something very intriguing with his fingers that further confirmed his point.

Just when things were really getting interesting, Nikos's phone buzzed. His private phone.

"Ugh," Olivia moaned. "Bad timing. Bad, bad timing."

"Hold that thought," Nikos muttered into her ear, then turned his attention to the phone. "Ya?"

It was Bryson.

"It's ready? Great, can't wait to see it. Yeah, we'll watch it right now."

He put the phone down, and Olivia turned to Nikos curiously.

"He's got the first cut done?"

"Yes…let me find the clicker…"

They clambered over one another, shifting around, digging under the cushions for the always elusive device.

Nikos found it and eagerly navigated to the new content Bryson had produced.

The video opened with a shot of a low-slung race car speeding along a road twisting through rugged mountains, along a coastal vista. The scene cut to the car screaming past the iconic Hollywood sign, the letters illuminating one at a time as it passed.

"Oh, that's a nice touch," Olivia murmured.

The camera angle changed to capture the car zooming under a blue-sky canopy lined with palms. Finally, it stopped in front of the Santa Monica Pier.

The words *Welcome to the Los Angeles Grand Prix* appeared, accompanied by a voiceover Nikos had recorded a month earlier. He invited investors to participate in an exciting new project, with seed money from Leonikaros Racing, that would expand Formula 1 in the United States. In addition to an LA circuit, the initiative would create driving academies in three other US cities where races were held. Scholarships would be available to encourage both boys and girls to take up the sport.

"This is really good," Nikos confirmed. "I think the investors are going to be impressed."

"It's so exciting to see it coming together," Olivia agreed.

"It is happening because you and my sister are a formidable management team, plus our Swiss gurus on financials…"

"And what about you?" Olivia teased. "Do you think you are just the pretty face of Leonikaros Racing…?"

"Everybody has a role." Nikos laughed.

"Seriously, though," Olivia said, "Nikos, this is awesome. I'm so proud of you for pushing for this dream. It was your idea and your drive that pulled it all together. It's incredible."

He didn't respond, but she could tell her compliment pleased him. She knew the transition from being a driver hadn't been as difficult as he'd feared, but there were still times he missed the sheer adrenaline of competing at the highest level. But their new project would keep him connected and allow him to expand the sport he loved. And if he needed speed-driven adrenaline, he always had the motorcycle.

"Did you set the date for the initial investors meeting in New York?" Nikos asked.

"Yep, it will be in early October, then we can fly back to Pittsburgh for the wedding. My mother has a full itinerary planned. We are going to be busy every day through Thanksgiving. Then we can head over to Europe for Christmas with Mags and Stefano. Spend New Year's in Greece with your family. And then..."

"Our honeymoon at last." He squeezed her enthusiastically.

"Someplace on the beach..." Olivia sighed. Nikos was in charge of planning the honeymoon. He was keeping the details a surprise, but Olivia knew it included sun and salt water. "Give me a hint."

"Nope." He kissed her. His hand drifted back under her robe.

"Please..."

"Okay, just a few little hints," he conceded as his fingers traced lazy circles over her skin. "It will involve complete privacy and a warm ocean. We won't have to wear bathing suits when we swim or do anything else we like to do outside..."

"I do enjoy activities outside without bathing suits..." Olivia teased.

"I wonder what you have in mind...?"

"Use your imagination."

Nikos's grin left little doubt that he knew exactly what she liked to do outside.

Thinking of their wedding and honeymoon

plans, Olivia sighed contentedly. "Nikos, do you know your mom already has everyone in your family baking cookies for the reception? They will ship them to my mom for the cookie table. There will be a billion cookies."

"I did hear about that. I'm making the *kourabiedes*."

He had taken up baking with a passion. The man did nothing halfway.

Olivia laughed. "You know, traditionally it isn't the groom who does the baking."

"I need to make sure there are cookies at our wedding that don't contain peanut butter," he insisted. "Also, if it hadn't been for cookies, we wouldn't be together now."

And that was the last thing he said to Olivia for quite some time because he was too busy proving to her how sweet life could be.

* * * * *

Bridesmaid's Fast-Track Fling

is Elle Brown's debut title for Harlequin. Look out for more books from Elle Brown, coming soon!